Still Small Voice

Book Two of the Towers of Light Series

Allen Brokken

"And he said, Go forth, and stand upon the mount before the LORD. And, behold, the LORD passed by, and a great and strong wind rent the mountains, and brake in pieces the rocks before the LORD; but the LORD was not in the wind: and after the wind an earthquake; but the LORD was not in the earthquake:

And after the earthquake a fire; but the LORD was not in the fire: and after the fire a still small voice."

1 Kings 19:9-13

Still Small Voice – Book 2 of the Towers of Light Series
Copyright © 2020 Allen Brokken
Written by Allen Brokken
Edited by S.D. Grimm
Cover by LoriAnn Weldon of Magpie Designs
Version 1.1
ISBN 9780578674322

Dedication

To the many teachers and mentors in my life, who always impressed upon me that I was good, but I could be great.

Contents

WARNING! This is Book 2 in the Series

The action-packed and suspenseful Towers of Light series is meant to be enjoyed in order, from the first book until the last. However, if you just can't wait to start your adventure, here's a brief summary of the previous books.

Book 1: *Light of Mine*

Darkness is spreading through Zoura. Beyond the borders of the Heathlands, innocent animals are being transformed into monsters and good men into pawns of the Dark One. A frontier family takes up the call to defend the Heathlands by building the Tower of Light. Soon after, Father joins the Mighty Mercenaries to help them hold back the darkness on the front but then disappears. Mother soon follows, leaving the children in the care of their Parson and church family, or so she believes.

Alone on the farm, twelve-year-old Lauren and her brave little brothers, Aiden (nine) and Ethan (five) must guard the Tower of Light that will guide both parents home. But when the hooded Knight Protector is caught trespassing on the farm and a new bishop removes the parson from the church, confusion pervades their close-knit community. He orders the Acolyte of the Violet Order to watch over the children, much to their dismay.

With little else but the aid of a trio of blessed pets, three holy weapons, and their growing faith, Lauren, Aiden, and Ethan must discern whom to trust while under the watchful eye of the Acolyte, who does not seem as trustworthy as he appears. A battle ensues, and the children must defend the Tower of Light. In their hour of need, the Knight Protector encourages them to shine the Light of their faith to defeat the Bishop and his acolytes.

1. Prologue

"The Darkness is winning." Father pushed back his half-eaten plate on the rectangular oak table he, his parents, and his brother had gathered around for lunch. The corners of his hazel eyes showed deep wrinkles, and, for a man of thirty-eight, too much gray sprinkled his tightly cropped dark brown hair.

"Despite the best efforts of many, I see the Darkness dropping like a cloak across the Heathlands. Each trip is getting more dangerous. I'm afraid my children will grow up without a father." He slumped back in the large oak armchair at the foot of the table, which was made to accommodate the big men of the family, armor and all. This was going to be a hard conversation. *Was it the right time?*

"You are of the Light, son, and so is your young family." Grandmother busied herself, clearing the table. "The Darkness cannot stand in your presence while the Tower of Light shines over you."

"Ma, I'll take that." Father's older brother got up from his oak armchair and took the dishes from her. "You visit, seein' as he's just in fer lunch. All this darkness talk ain't fer me anyhow." He was as tall as Father but far more muscular and rounder in the middle. His sandy-blond hair was as long and unruly as his beard.

Grandmother brushed a lock of gray hair out of her face and then wiped her hands on the gingham apron she wore over her simple denim smock dress. She favored her right knee as she sat back down at her seat on the corner of the table next to Grandfather.

"I believe what you say with all of my heart. But the enemy is crafty. I can't begin to explain all of the subtle corruptions I've seen in the world." Father shook his head in dismay. "How do I describe the horror I've seen to those who have always lived in the Light?"

Father strained under the weight of his armor as he stood. "The Dark One is the master of this world." He motioned open-palmed toward the window. "I've seen fields like that corrupted by the Darkness, turned gray and sickly, the animals becoming feral." He began to pace. *Will they believe me if I share the worst?* "Beyond the Heathlands, there are tales of the Bjorn Born and the bears at war with each other and other tales of a great thorn wall holding back the Light in the south."

"Is that so?" Grandfather said as he peeled an orange with a slight shake in his work-worn hands. What little gray hair he had left was cropped shorter than Father's, and his wrinkles were deeper, but otherwise, they were the spitting image of one another.

Uncle returned to the table and sat back in his chair to Father's right. "I always thought the Bjorn Born were just a myth. Sounds like someone telling ghost stories to me."

"Myth or no, what I've seen is that the Darkness is more powerful than we give it credit for." Father rubbed his weary eyes. *Brother, if only you could see the Light.*

"Son, it sounds like you're trying to carry the weight of the world. How can we help?" Grandfather raised both hands, palms up.

Father put a hand to his mouth and rubbed it down his red goatee as he paused his pacing. *He's right. I must share this burden.* He turned and looked gravely at his parents. "I really didn't want to put any of this on you. We built the tower to shine a way home for me. However, with the Darkness spreading, I worry something will happen to take their mother and me despite our best efforts."

Uncle shook his head slightly as he slowly stroked his bushy blond beard. "Sounds like you ain't so sure of all that Good Book talk after all."

"I get it. You're a skeptic, but whether you buy into it or not, I tell you a battle between the Darkness and the Light is coming." Father leaned forward and stared directly into Uncle's eyes. *Please don't make this harder than it has to be.*

"What about them high and mighty mercenaries you joined? I wouldn't trust one of them any further than I could throw them. Ain't they got the muscle to keep you safe?" Uncle flexed his right biceps. "I never much trusted them anyhow."

"Muscle isn't going to be enough to stem the tide of evil." Father paused, letting his words sink in. "If I fall, I need to know my children will have a safe place to grow up and reflect the Light."

Uncle looked down and away. That did it. He was listening now.

"Originally, I thought to have them go to the garrison in Blooming Glen. Being surrounded by the Mighty Mercenaries and their training would be the way to ensure they were protected," Father continued as he sat back in his chair. "However, not all of them are of the Light, and the garrison itself seems to be in a state of . . . gray. Neither really committed to the Light nor Darkness."

Mother spoke, quoting the scriptures with authority, "So, because you are lukewarm—neither hot nor cold—I am about to spit you out of my mouth."

"Exactly. Since I just don't know who to trust, I must ask, if something happens to their mother and me, can you take them in?" Father exhaled, and the last bit of tension in his body left him.

Grandmother sat forward in her seat, "Of course. How could you think we would say otherwise?"

Father looked down at his hands. *How can I explain? Of course, they would take the children in.* "You have so much going on with your congregation, and you aren't getting any younger. Plus, I know it's too far of a journey for Grandfather to go get them," Father explained.

"Don't worry 'bout that. I'll go get them if it comes to that," Uncle declared with a note of finality.

"Really?" Father stood straight up and stared wide-eyed at his elder brother.

Uncle rose, "Blood is thicker 'n water. I don't care much for the idea of some high Mighty Mercenary raisin' those kids. Those young'uns are *MY* Nibbles." He rounded the table and put a hand on Father's shoulder.

"That's settled then." Father beamed with gratitude. "It's important that if you get word they're in danger, you need to go with haste to get them."

Father turned and got his dark brown leather pack from the corner of the room. He pulled a sealed roll of paper from an outer pocket of the pack and handed it to Uncle. "This writ will show any who ask, including my children, that these are my wishes. Our parson will have a copy to verify your claim. If something should change, I'll send you both a new writ."

Uncle accepted the writ and gave his brother a one-armed hug.

Grandmother looked at her sons with pride in her eyes. "That's settled then. Let's pray this is never needed."

2. Awakening

Mama is trapped in a dark place! Ethan woke with a start. His dream was so real. The room Mama was in was so scary. But she was happy; she saw their light. *Mama was so proud I shined my light.* They needed to go to Blooming Glen to shine it over the whole wide world. Mama said so in the dream! *Can we do it? Who would help us?*

"Sissy! Aiden! I saw Mama and Daddy! They were in a dark place. We have to help!" Ethan shook his sleeping siblings through the patchwork quilt.

"Ughhh. No wakey. Tired." Aiden groaned and pulled the blanket they shared over his head.

Ethan tugged on the quilt, but Aiden held fast. With a growl of determination, Ethan shook his sister. "Sissy!"

"What, E? I'm so tired." Lauren moved her arm such that her shoulder covered her ear, and her forearm shielded her eyes.

"Mama! I saw Mama!" the force of his voice echoed in the cramped loft.

Lauren sat up, pulling the quilt off Aiden. She rubbed her eyes and brushed stray strands of her light brown hair out of her face. "What did you say?"

"In my dream, I saw Mama. She saw our light!" he beamed as he pointed out the window at the Tower of Light.

"E . . . Slow down." Aiden pushed himself up onto an elbow.

"Mama, I saw Mama. She is locked up in some dark place." Ethan shuddered. "She said we have to shine the Light over the whole wide world like the song. 'Bad men are coming,' Mama said. We need to go!"

I'm going to need my shield to shine my light! Ethan hopped out of bed and looked around for his shield. "And I saw Daddy! Well, I think so. He is locked in a mask."

"OK, OK, E!" Lauren sat up on the side of the bed and then stretched her arms. "I know you see things in your dreams. I believe you. Just give us a minute to wake up and get oriented."

Ethan paused as he noticed Lauren was still in her work dress from the day before. It had smears of mud and small spots of blood on it. *Nicolas! He was such a good friend. Why did he have to die?* Tears welled up in his eyes.

"E, what is it, little buddy?" Lauren got out of bed and knelt to put an arm around his shoulder.

Ethan looked down at his own filthy hands and clothes while the tears flowed freely. "Nicolas."

Lauren reached into her pocket and pulled out a red paisley handkerchief, and wiped the tears and grime off his face. "Why don't we go down and wash up, and you can tell us about your dream."

7

"What's that smell?" Aiden pushed past them to the ladder. "It smells like breakfast, and I'm starved."

"Let's go see." Lauren grabbed Aiden's shoulder and turned him to face her. "We need to take clean clothes with us as we go down. We'll get a bite to eat and then change."

Ethan snuffled up his tears while Lauren and Aiden grabbed some clothes from the trunk. *I'm hungry too. Nicolas wouldn't want me to be hungry.*

Lauren looked back at Ethan with big eyes and a goofy full-teeth smile. It forced a huffing laugh out of him as she handed him clean clothes.

Aiden got to the ladder first, followed by Lauren. Ethan came last, eyeing his shield leaning against their clothes chest for a moment, but decided he couldn't carry it and his clothes.

He followed his nose to the kitchen, where he found Knight Protector without his armor in a long linen shirt and leather breeches. He was standing over a cast-iron skillet and cooking flapjacks in bacon fat. A pile of bacon sat on the table.

He turned around and visibly winced at the sight of the children. "Oh, children. You have been through so much."

Ethan ran over to him. The grizzled old knight took a knee and hugged Ethan as Ethan began to sob again about the loss of his friend. *Nicolas saved Sparkle Frog and Sissy and Aiden. Why did he have to die?*

8

The scent of burning dough broke through Ethan's despair and activated a strong grumbling in his stomach. Through his tears, Ethan saw Lauren step up to the skillet and flip the flapjacks. *Sissy is so good. She always does the right thing.*

Ethan's sobs subsided, and Knight Protector stood back up. He patted Ethan on his head. "Children, wash your hands and go ahead and start eating."

Ethan looked down at his palms and saw the blood again. *Nicolas.*

The tears began to well up, but Lauren took his hands in hers. "We're such a mess. Let me help you get washed up."

In the morning light of the kitchen, Lauren looked completely out of sorts. *I bet Sissy's embarrassed for being a mess with Knight Protector here.* His eyes darted around, hoping to quickly find the soap and a bucket.

"There will be time for a proper bath and clean clothes later," The knight soothed, placing a bucket of water at the children's feet. An oblong bar of lye soap had sunk to the bottom of the bucket. "We must eat and talk. There is so much more going on here than you know, children."

Ethan knelt with Aiden and Lauren around the bucket, and they washed their hands up to their elbows. The water turned brown, and the soap stung, but his hands were clean. Knight Protector handed Lauren a towel, and she dried the boys' hands after drying hers.

"There are things you should know. . ." Knight Protector paused, staring out the window toward the tower. He paused for so long that Ethan turned to see if there was something out there.

Knight Protector finally spoke again, "I just don't know what is appropriate. I have spent my life in service to the realm. I believe our conversation last night was the most I've spoken to children in a decade."

Ethan was hungry and wondered where Knight Protector was going with this.

Knight Protector continued, "This is all so very complicated. But it is clear you are all clever and keep your own counsel on what is best." The warrior rubbed the top of his head.

Ethan winced. *We really conked him in his wonkus last night.*

"You will not just obey me because I am your elder." The old knight looked at each of the children staring into their eyes. "With the deception of the bishop and even my own behavior, it has to be difficult for you to trust anyone. Oh ... where to begin." Knight Protector sighed.

"Pray!" Ethan blurted out. He had a plate of bacon and flapjacks in front of him, and his stomach was aching.

"What?" Knight Protector sat back in his chair, wide-eyed at this.

"You said you didn't know where to begin. Daddy always says, when you don't know what to do, pray." Ethan folded his hands together. "Plus, we can't eat if we don't pray, and I'm starving."

"You are right, of course. This is your home and your table. Would you want to ask for the Lord's blessing for us?" Knight Protector asked.

"OK," Ethan bowed his head. "Dear God, bless this food, help the knight tell us things, and please give Nicolas a hug. We miss him. Amen."

"Amen" was repeated around the table.

The conversation halted for a few moments while the children shoveled food into their mouths. Ethan was glad he didn't get the burned flapjack; his were done just right.

Aiden was the first one to clear his plate. "Can you tell us what is really going on, Knight Protector, sir?"

"Well, son, that's probably a tale that would take weeks to tell. I think it best if I just start with when you first met me at Sunday services." Knight Protector set his fork down and placed his hands flat on the table.

"Darkness is encroaching from the east. The Heathlands have been free from the Darkness cloaking the rest of Zoura, but in recent weeks it seemed to be advancing. I was sent to spy here."

This confused Ethan. He thought spies were bad guys. Daddy always talked about finding spies in the dark woods.

Knight Protector continued, "I suspected the bishop, and his brood had something to do with it, but I wasn't really sure until last night. I was under orders to scout and report, not engage."

Ethan stopped eating and leaned forward, intent on the story. *Oh, he was spying on the bishop.*

"If you recall that day in the church, I wasn't just there to stir up things with the bishop. I was also there to check on the three of you." Knight Protector pointed his index finger at each of them.

How did Knight Protector know about them? Ethan shoved another piece of bacon into his mouth.

As if in answer to Ethan's unspoken thoughts, Knight Protector continued, "Your father was a protégé of mine in the Mighty Mercenaries. He asked me to ensure you were safely taken to Blooming Glen if anything happened to him."

Blooming Glen. That's where Mama said to go in my dream. Ethan was on the verge of interrupting but noticed the way Lauren and Aiden were listening intently, so he thought he should hear the rest of the story first.

The knight protector leaned forward, "I expected to meet with the parson to make the arrangements, but with the bishop in charge, I decided I needed to finish my investigation first."

Lauren held her palm out to Knight Protector, "Wait a second. You say Father wanted us to go to Blooming Glen?

That can't be right. We have a writ with Father's seal that says we're to go to Grandma's if something happens."

"Yeah, and what's this scout and report nonsense?" Aiden waved his hands in the air. "You're a knight protector. If you knew bad stuff was going on, why didn't you stop it?"

Aiden's indignation stoked a fire in Ethan's heart that overshadowed his questions about Blooming Glen, "Yeah, why didn't you just conk their wonkuses and lock them up?"

Knight Protector leaned back in his chair and held his hands up submissively. "Now, children, I'm very sorry for all of the pain you have gone through. But it's just not as simple as 'conking wonkuses.' You know that from your own experience."

Lauren nodded. "Boys, we should hear him out."

Aiden sat back in his seat, and Ethan followed suit.

Knight Protector moved his knife to draw lines through the syrup on his plate. "The Darkness can be very powerful. It spreads in stealthy ways."

Ethan knelt on his chair to see better.

"If we just attack it directly . . ." Knight Protector wiped his knife along the path of the lines he'd just drawn, and the syrup oozed around the plate, "it will slink away and return by a less obvious path."

Ethan was enthralled by the example. *Oooo, the Darkness is sneaky.*

The old warrior picked up the edge of his plate and tilted it. The syrup began to pool. "However, the Darkness' followers tend to get overconfident from time to time, and we can catch them unaware." He grabbed a spoon in his other hand and scooped up the syrup, and ate it.

That made Ethan and his siblings laugh. The giggles reduced the tension that had been tightening up Ethan's whole body.

The knight took a drink, "That's how we make a real difference. Besides, I'm only one man and not as spry as I used to be." He pulled on the length of his gray beard for emphasis. "Better to be seen as an addled, harmless old man than a threat when you don't yet understand who your enemy is or what their powers are. It also encourages them to become overconfident."

Ethan raised his eyebrows in surprise at how wise the knight protector was.

"That all makes sense, but I still don't understand what you were saying about Blooming Glen." Lauren pointed toward her parents' room. "We have a writ that looks real that says we're to go to Grandma's house."

"That is an old instruction." The knight let out a sigh. "Your father gave me two copies of a new writ."

This reminded Ethan of his dream, and he began looking for an opportunity to interrupt.

The knight protector continued, "I went to the Mercenaries' outpost to have a messenger deliver the new documents. Unfortunately, the Dandelion Acolyte we fought yesterday was acting as a page there."

Ethan's mouth dropped. The Dandelion Acolyte had disappeared into the woods after the battle last night. *Could he be outside listening in?*

"I believe he intercepted the documents to keep you from going to Blooming Glen and lighting another Tower of Light if your father and your mother went missing." A deep scowl spread across the knight protector's face. "I believe your mother has been captured by the forces of Darkness. So, I must follow your father's wishes in this."

Finally! I can tell about my dream, "She is captured. The Darkness has her, and she's locked up in a dark place." Ethan slapped both hands on the table for emphasis.

"What? How do you know that?" Knight Protector's eyes went wide as he looked at Ethan intently.

The thought that the Dandelion Acolyte might be outside listening came back to Ethan. He stood on his chair, rested his hands on the table, and whispered, "I have dreams. She is locked up, but she saw our light last night. She said we must go light the other towers. She said to go to Blooming Glen and shine our light."

Lauren raised an eyebrow as she leaned in. "E, why are you whispering?"

Ethan rolled his eyes at Lauren and whispered even more quietly, "The yellow acolyte could be outside spying, of course." Ethan couldn't believe they hadn't all thought of that.

"Oh!" Lauren looked around as if suddenly unsure of herself.

Knight Protector put a hand on Lauren's shoulder, "I'm sure he's long gone by now. Regardless, Ethan's dream confirms what your father told me. I'm sure he and your mother discussed such things."

Aiden knelt on his chair and leaned in to whisper, "But what about the paper? Daddy said we should go to Grandma's house."

Ethan realized Aiden wasn't so sure that the yellow acolyte wasn't listening in.

"Grandma's wise and knows about the Light," Aiden pointed to the tower out the window. "She would know more about our weapons and what we're meant to do." Aiden flushed red from his neck to the top of his head. "We should go there first and see what she says about Blooming Glen!" He banged his fist on the table for emphasis as he sat up straight and confident.

"Perhaps," Knight Protector looked out the kitchen window towards the Tower of Light. "The Darkness is spreading fast. Your parents' disappearance is proof of that. I'm not sure there's time for your plan." He looked down at his hands and shook his head. "Children, I need some time to think. Maybe some chores to keep the mind free and the hands busy will add some clarity."

"Chores!" the boys whined in unison.

"Chores." Lauren was already on her feet, picking up plates from the table. "It won't take long, and then we can decide what to do."

Ethan wasn't looking forward to chores. But at least he wouldn't have to go to the woods to get water since Aiden had fixed the windmill. Ethan still thought the yellow acolyte might be out there, waiting to attack them.

3. Amnesia

The teenage boy awoke in the heat of the noonday sun.
Mud caked his tan denim pants from the knees down. A
leather belt with a brass buckle in the shape of a dandelion
cinched his slacks tight. He stared at the intricate buckle,
having no memory of it. He was lying in a small patch of
thick, green grass under the canopy of a wooded glen. A
stream gently burbled to his right. Where was this place?
Why couldn't he remember?

With the sun directly overhead, he couldn't get a sense
of direction, nor could he see any landmarks while on the
ground. He was painfully hungry and thirsty. *I need a
drink.*

As he sat up, searing pain exploded in his forehead. It
slowly faded to a dull throb as he pulled his knees to his
chest. He held his forehead in both hands and felt a painful
bump right above his eyebrows. It hurt him more as he
touched it. He squeezed his eyes shut to the agony and let
out a low groan.

The pain subsided to a rhythmic throbbing in time with
his heartbeat. He slowly opened his eyes and saw a pair of
mud-encrusted sandals tangled in the grass where his feet
had been.

The ache of ravenous hunger and thirst finally exceeded
the pain in his throbbing head. He scooted on the ground to
the sandals and put them on. With his feet protected, he
prepared to stand up to walk to the stream. He looked

around for something he could lean on to help him stand, but moving his head made him feel like the flesh on the back of his neck was cracking open. He gingerly reached back and touched his neck. His taught skin felt dry and flaky from just above his shoulders to his hairline. *Was it a cut?*

Flakes of dried dirt came off of his fingers—not the blood he expected. He sighed, then dislodged as much mud as he could from his neck and shaggy black hair.

He scanned the rest of his body. *Why was there no mud on his chest?*

A wave of hunger and thirst passed over him. *Need water.* He steeled his resolve to stand up. He brought up one knee and placed his foot firmly on the ground. With that sudden motion, a wave of vertigo came over him. He fell forward onto his hands and knees and stayed still, waiting for the feeling to subside.

Realizing he might fall over if he stood, he crawled slowly toward the stream, pausing occasionally. After a few moments of struggling with the pain and vertigo, he made it to the edge of the stream.

At first, the boy lay down with his head and shoulder hanging over the stream. Then he tried to cup water in his hand and lap it up from there. *Too slow.* He pushed himself farther forward to drink directly from the stream. Suddenly the overhang gave way, and his whole head went underwater.

He had the presence of mind to catch a big breath before he went in. The cool water was a shock to his system at first, and then it acted as a soothing balm on his aching head. He stayed under as long as he could stand it and then scooted his body back and lifted his head out of the creek. Vertigo washed over him, and he collapsed on the bank.

When the wave passed, he felt his forehead. The bump wasn't as pronounced, and overall, he felt much better. He scooped up water in his hands and eventually slaked his thirst. *Need food.*

He caught sight of a blackberry bush a few feet upstream. He crept to the bush and quickly stripped the closest branch, enduring the thorn pricks. He greedily stuffed the berries into his mouth. While it wasn't a full meal, his hunger abated to a reasonable level.

He crawled back to the edge of the stream and washed off the remaining mud. When that was done, he stared off into the horizon. *Where am I?*

The last memory he had was entering the new youth tent at the chapel in Loggerton and passing through some smoke. Now he was here.

He didn't know how he ended up here. Someone must have waylaid him. *But who?* When he figured that out, somebody was going to pay, that was for sure. For now, he couldn't stay here.

Something about *here* was off. The sun was straight up. However, a light almost as bright as the sun seemed to be coming through the trees. He couldn't tell what the source was. It had to be man-made. As good a place as any to start looking for answers.

He steeled himself to stand up and then worked his way onto his knees. He didn't experience vertigo, but the throbbing in his head returned. He paused for a moment before clenching his teeth and standing up. The pounding accelerated from a dull thud to a loud roar as he walked toward the light.

He reached a thick patch of grass, stumbled to his knees, and then lay down on the lush carpet of cool grass. It felt soft and inviting in comparison to the pain of trying to walk. His head thudded mercilessly. *Whoever did this to me will pay! They'll pay dearly.* The pounding in his head reached a crescendo, and he passed into unconsciousness.

4. The Decision

Aiden returned from his chores, relieved that Knight Protector was right about the yellow acolyte not skulking about. However, he was frustrated that Knight Protector thought they should go to Blooming Glen. *Of course, we should go to Grandma's house. She's wise, and she taught Daddy about the Light. She'll know what we should really do.*

Aiden set the logs he was carrying next to the oven in the kitchen and heard voices in the great room. He stepped in through the door and noticed Lauren and Ethan tidying up around the fireplace. Knight Protector was sitting in Father's chair. "Come sit, children. Let's talk this through."

Lauren and Ethan sat crisscross applesauce on the woven rug in front of Knight Protector. Lauren's black kitten with white paws, Meow Meow, came to sit in her lap.

However, Aiden remained standing. "What do you mean, 'perhaps' we should go to Grandma's house? We're GOING to Grandma's house."

Lauren's and Ethan's eyes got big at this declaration.

The knight protector steepled his fingers as he spoke directly to Aiden. "For the three of you to defeat a pack of hell hounds, two acolytes, and a censer-wielding bishop is no simple feat. It's clear the Lord was with the three of you." Aiden puffed up his chest as he remembered the look on the bishop's face as Aiden had cut open the sack containing the Lantern of Light.

"However," Knight Protector continued, "it is also clear you didn't really know much about the tower or your weapons. I recall you rushing into battle last night, and it didn't seem like much of a plan. Is that right?" Knight Protector's raised eyebrows reminded Aiden of Father's when he caught Aiden telling a tall tale.

This made Aiden uncomfortable, and he felt like he should explain himself. "Well, I knew my sword starts fires and cuts metal and stuff. Sissy can make people forget with her spear. I guess we didn't really know what E's shield did. But we know now. It made the bad dogs go poof." Aiden brought the tips of the fingers on both hands together and then pulled his hands apart.

"Poof is right!" Ethan agreed, making the same motion.

"Yes, Knight Protector, sir, we can do some amazing things when the Lord wants us to," Lauren nodded. "But that power only comes when it seems like the Lord wants us to have it."

Aiden let out a big sigh, "That's why we should go to Grandma's house. She's wise. She knows all about this stuff."

"I understand your grandmother is wise. That is why I say 'perhaps.'" Knight Protector sat back in his chair and folded his hands together. "Your father was very clear, and I saw it in writing. Lighting a tower just like the one here in

Blooming Glen was essential to holding back the Darkness."

Aiden faltered for a moment. If Daddy wrote it, he had to mean it. It had to be the right thing. But Daddy was a good teacher. He wouldn't just leave them with all this power with no explanation. "When did Daddy give you the paper?"

"Well, just a few days ago." Knight Protector cocked his head. "Why would that matter?"

"He was on his way home when he disappeared." Aiden let out a deep breath to compose himself. "What if he expected to come home to explain things but never made it?"

"And?" a quizzical look passed over the Knight Protector's face. "Why would that matter?"

"You said yourself we don't really know about our weapons and the tower," Aiden pointed at the knight protector for emphasis, "right?"

Knight Protector nodded, "Yes, I did say that."

Aiden shrugged his shoulders and raised his hands. "Who in Blooming Glen is as wise as Grandma?"

Knight Protector sat in silence for a moment, "Children, is going to your grandmother's house what the Lord is asking you to do?"

Ethan's face contorted in concentration. "Hmmm." He was squeezing his eyes closed and mouth so hard his face was starting to turn red.

Aiden let out a huff. "E, it doesn't work like that."

Ethan exhaled, and his shoulders fell as his face relaxed, "How do you know how it works for me?"

"I just know that when it was time to cut down the Darkness tower, I felt like God was nudging my brain," Aiden tapped the side of his head. "Then the fire started on my sword. I didn't sit there growling like I was concentrating."

"I agree with Aiden, E," Lauren nodded towards Aiden. "It was like the Good Book says. It was a 'still small voice' that fills you with power."

"Where does the Good Book say that, Sissy? Can you read it? I want to know about that voice," Ethan pointed to the Good Book on the table next to Father's chair.

"I don't know exactly where that is in the Good Book, E." Lauren set Meow Meow aside and stood.

Knight Protector cleared his throat, "And he said, 'Go forth, and stand upon the mount before the Lord.' And, behold, the Lord passed by, and a great and strong wind rent the mountains and break in pieces the rocks before the Lord; but the Lord was not in the wind: and after the wind an earthquake; but the Lord was not in the earthquake: And after the earthquake a fire; but the Lord was not in the fire:

and after the fire, a still small voice," recited Knight Protector. "Is that the one you mean, Lauren?"

Lauren sat back down and retrieved her kitten. "That's how I remember the evening that I threw the spear. A lot was going on outside, and there was a loud ruckus. But it was the 'still small voice' that directed that I should get up and look out the window."

That's how Aiden remembered his sword lit up. It was a nudge to go do something, not a booming voice from the heavens.

"You told me to shine my light," Ethan pointed at Knight Protector, "but my remebery told me to sing the song. Is that the small voice? Because that's what Mama's message felt like."

Knight Protector turned to Lauren, "That sounds right. It has also been so in my own life. It was that 'still small voice' that prompted me to watch over you children these past few days and to seek and find the source of the Darkness in these lands."

Aiden wasn't buying it. *I don't think the Lord would let the bad stuff go on if a warrior like Knight Protector could do something about it.* Aiden balled his fists and put them on his hips. "But, if the small voice told you to find the Darkness machine, why didn't you knock it down before we got there?"

Knight Protector leaned forward in his chair with his hands on the arms and looked straight at Aiden. "It was the Spirit's promptings that helped me to find the Darkness generator. Then the 'still small voice' told me to wait and see. And low and behold, I saw a young boy wield the sword of Gabriel and smite the Darkness. That was a most glorious sight indeed."

"The sword of Gabriel? You mean the archangel Gabriel from the Good Book?" Lauren blurted out unexpectedly. This caused Aiden to take a step back.

"Well, maybe not 'the' sword of Gabriel. It stands watch over the garden. But a fiery sword of the type only wielded by the angels." Knight Protector patted the Good Book to emphasize his point.

Aiden's mind swirled at the thought that his sword may have been wielded by angels. "Wow! I never thought of it like that."

Ethan's face fell, and his lower lip stuck out, "Aiden has an angel sword! I want an angel sword."

Knight Protector turned to Ethan with a hard look. "Son, it wasn't a sword that won your battle last night. It was the shielding light that you carried with you. I would not be so quick to dismiss the great gift the Lord granted you."

Ethan looked down at the floor and picked at a loose thread in the rug. "You're right, I guess."

Ethan's dream said we should go to Blooming Glen, and you say the same thing. But I read Daddy's paper, and it said we should go to Grandma's house." The kitten began to squirm, and she set him down. She turned to Knight

Protector and pointed at him, "What happens if we pick the wrong one?"

Knight Protector's eyes narrowed, "Well if the Lord calls you to something and you don't do it, there are usually consequences. Do you know the story about the prophet and the leviathan?"

Ethan spread his arms wide. "He got eaten by a big fish! I don't want to be eaten by a big fish!" His eyes went wild. "We should go to Blooming Glen."

That made Aiden's blood boil. *This is hard enough as it is. Now he's getting Ethan all riled up.* Aiden was getting frustrated with the whole conversation. "Why are you so against going to Grandma's house first? She's wise, and she can help us know what to do."

Knight Protector exhaled a deep breath. "I'm not against seeking your grandmother's wisdom. However, the forces of Darkness have your parents and are growing in power every day. I put it to you, is the Holy Spirit telling you that's where you need to go right now? Because I think that's what your brother is saying."

Aiden didn't expect to be put on the spot like that. "Hey, that's not fair. I don't have some kind of lever to turn it on and off."

"You are right. The 'still small voice' doesn't come on demand. Just take a moment, calm down, and search your feelings." Knight Protector ran his hand down his beard and remained focused intently on Aiden.

I don't feel like I did when my sword caught fire. Aiden searched his thoughts and feelings deeper. *We've lost Mama and Daddy. Do we have to lose our home too? Grandma's house is like ours; I don't want to go to a strange place.* Tears began to pool in his eyes, threatening to flow over.

Knight Protector's face softened, and he looked like Grandpa for just a moment. "I know you all would be safer in Blooming Glen than anywhere else." He got up and knelt on one knee in front of Aiden and put his hands on the boy's shoulders. "I also know that's where your father said it was imperative to light the tower there. I believe that if we take any other path, there will be dire consequences."

Aiden looked down at his feet. Going to Grandma's house would feel better than going to a strange place. But that wasn't a reason not to obey Daddy's plan and Ethan's dream, especially since he said it was the 'still small voice.'

Knight Protector pulled a paisley handkerchief out of his pocket and wiped the tears from Aiden's eyes. "So, young Aiden, what do you say?"

Aiden snuffed back his sorrow and looked up at Knight Protector. "I don't hear the 'still small voice' about this, but it seems like that's what Ethan's dream was. It says to go to Blooming Glen, and I guess I believe you. That's what Daddy told you to do. So, that's where we should go."

Knight Protector patted Aiden on the head. "That's settled then." Knight Protector stood and began gathering his gear. "I have to leave to make preparation for you to

travel to Blooming Glen. I'll send helpers with my seal."
He turned and showed them a symbol on his belt.

Aiden was frozen in shock. A wave of fear gripped him.
"You're leaving? What if the bishop's people come back?"
Aiden looked to his siblings for support.

Ethan got up and ran to Knight Protector, grabbing his
hand. "What if the yellow acolyte comes back?"

Knight Protector picked Ethan up and looked him in the
eyes. "In the light of the day and with the tower locked up
tight, you have nothing to fear from the Dark One."

Knight Protector gave Ethan a hug and set him down.
"There's no other way to do this. You are safest here in the
light of the tower. I'll send helpers soon."

With that, the knight protector left. Seeing Ethan's
reaction, Aiden steeled himself to support his younger
brother. Aiden believed the light of the tower would protect
them, but he also feared that the yellow acolyte was still out
there, somewhere. *That's somebody who's going to get
some consequences if I see him again.* So, he strapped on
his sword belt, just in case.

5. Restless Slumber

The youth lay flat in the deep grass with the canopy of the woods shading him from the worst of the afternoon sun. He twitched at irregular intervals as his mind swirled with images, both foreign and familiar.

His unconscious brain was working overtime to retrieve even the most basic facts about himself, including his name. A particularly vivid scene came to him as the evening twilight came.

The vision began with his arm coming up reflexively as a blinding light blasted him. It was so powerful he had to take a step back and hold his eyes closed for a minute to make the spots disappear.

"Strife! Conflict! Kill that boy first!" Came a voice that seemed familiar called, but he couldn't place it at first. It sounded hoarse and was followed by grunts from exertion. His eyes were still clearing, so he couldn't see why.

He wanted to rub his eyes but realized he had a sword in his right hand. He used his left, and his eyes cleared in time to see the silhouette of two large beasts as they strode towards a little boy carrying a shield that was the source of the light. He could barely make out the boy from the brightness of the shield, but he heard him clear enough, "This little light of mine, I'm gonna let it shine."

Something about that boy and that song infuriated him. How dare this heathen claim the Light!

The hounds passed the visible threshold of the shadows into the bright light the shield was casting, and their bodies burst into flames. They reared back, but their forward momentum slammed them into the shield, and they vaporized.

The sight stunned him completely. What power that shield has! If I could take it from him, I would be unstoppable.

"Acolyte!" the hoarse voice called with a hint of desperation.

The dawning of identity returned. *Acolyte? I am an acolyte.*

The man ordered, "The shield is the key. We must outflank them and get behind the shield." He grabbed the acolyte by the shoulders and looked him in the eyes. "Fade back a few steps to the left, then circle from that side."

The acolyte moved into position and saw, just beyond the children, a black sphere crisscrossed with irregular cuts leaking a red light.

He remembered a flash from the youth pavilion in Loggerton. *The Censers are the vessels of the true light of knowledge. He must protect it.*

The acolyte focused on his target, the girl on the left, and charged. She stepped forward, spear at the ready. A blue-green aura brightened its tip and emphasized the point so that there was no way to avoid it. He poured on the speed, hoping to close the gap and run her over before she could throw.

With three paces to close the gap, the spear hit him like a mule kick to the chest. He flew backward and felt a crushing pain in the back of his head. I'll get you for this, you evil girl, and that shield will be mine. Then he lapsed into total darkness.

Lauren heard plates hitting the table as Ethan set it. When he was done, he asked, "Do you think Sparkle Frog will want to come with me to Blooming Glen?"

Lauren used a big fork to take a cured ham steak from the cast-iron skillet on the stove and place it on the cutting board. "I don't know about that." She was glad the knight protector was able to leave the provisions the parson sent with him. They were getting tired of oatmeal and eggs.

"I hope Daddy Duck will come too." Aiden was working the fire behind her. She could hear the familiar scrape of iron on brickwork.

Ethan moved to the other side of the counter from Lauren as she cut the ham steak. "Meow Meow has to come. We can't leave him here. He's a baby. He would get hungry."

As if to emphasize the point, Meow Meow sauntered out from under the counter and rubbed his black, furry body against Lauren's leg.

Task complete, Lauren set down the knife and handed the serving fork to Aiden. She picked up her kitten, and he flailed his white-tipped paws until she stroked his back. "Meow Meow is our pet."

She loved her kitten and knew the boys loved their special animals, but they were wild animals. "I don't know

34

how we'd bring them along without caging them. That's not really a fair thing to do to them, don't you think?"

"I know!" Ethan threw his hands into the air as if he had the best idea in the world, "What if we ask them?"

A slight giggle came out reflexively at Ethan's enthusiasm. Their animals all had special powers, but she didn't think understanding human language was one of them. While she thought about it, she took a crocheted hot pad and carried the fried green tomatoes in their cast-iron skillet to the table. "I don't think they really understand our words, Ethan."

Aiden finished putting the steaks on a serving plate and carried them to the table. "Maybe we should ask Knight Protector when he gets back."

Ethan's eyes got big, and he put his hands on his cheeks. "What if he says no?"

The thought turned Lauren's stomach in knots. Meow Meow was so little he couldn't survive on his own. Knight Protector wouldn't be that cruel. "We'll worry about that later. Right now, we need to eat."

Ethan stiffened for a moment, then sat compliantly in his chair, "OK, Sissy."

They all sat at the table and said a quick prayer, then dug in with gusto. Lauren watched the boys inhale their food. Despite the big breakfast, chores, and the little bit of packing they had done, really brought on an appetite.

She was eating at a more measured pace while pondering the fate of Sparkle Frog and Daddy Duck when a thought came to her. "Boys, we've been so busy we never did get cleaned up. Look at you two. You're a mess."

Ethan traded glances with Aiden over their empty plates, "Do we HAVE to take a bath?"

Lauren got up and grabbed the bar of lye soap from the kitchen counter. "You two take this and take a bath in the stream when you're done eating. Get some clean clothes to take with you. Don't get them soaked in the water."

"Yes, Ma'am," the boys said in unison with a salute. Aiden grabbed the soap, and they were off to the loft to get some clothes.

Lauren took a minute to put a pot of water on the stove, then returned to finish her lunch. She ate while mulling over arguments for taking their animals along. *Would the knight protector really leave Meow Meow behind?* The uncertainty drained the last of Lauren's appetite. She decided it would be better to be busy than to worry.

She cleaned up the table, added the hot water to a bucket that was one-third of the way full of cold water, and took it to her parents' room to wash up and change.

Being clean lifted her spirits for a moment, and she decided she should wash her clothes with the bathwater that was still hot. However, trying to clean the blood out of her dress reminded her of the loss of Nicolas. She sat down in the chair in the great room and cried.

Meow Meow must have sensed her feelings because he jumped up on the chair. He couldn't quite make the leap and got stuck with his front paws on top of the seam and his back paws scrambling to climb the rest of the way.

"Poor little kitty." Lauren sniffed through her tears as she picked up Meow Meow and looked the squirming kitten in the eyes. "What do you think, little guy? Can the chores wait a few minutes?"

"Meow. Meow," the tiny kitten squeaked out.

"That's what I thought you'd say." She put him in her lap and petted him until he purred. Her tears subsided as she and her kitten nodded off to sleep.

Lauren woke with a start to the sound of laughing and splashing outside.

Meow Meow was in a deep sleep on her lap. Lauren paused for a moment looking at how cute and peaceful the kitten's white face was. Then she remembered she had sent the boys to the pond to get cleaned up.

Oh no! The chores! She picked up Meow Meow as she stood. "What do you think, Meow Meow? Those boys must have decided to play in the horse trough instead of the creek."

She put Meow Meow on the floor. In a rush, she hurried through the kitchen and out the door, disgusted at the dirty dishes still sitting on the counter. When she stepped outside, she heard sloshing to her left and turned.

The boys were making a ruckus while actively scrubbing their dirty clothes in the wooden washtub on the porch.

Behind them, a huge man wearing a hooded cloak dismounted his horse.

"Boys!" Lauren rushed to them.

The boys were making so much noise that they didn't notice the man approaching from behind.

"What, Sissy?" Ethan asked with a hurt look. "We thought we did good."

"Behind you! Run!" Lauren barked as she tried to remember where their weapons were.

The boys turned and yelped as the large man stepped onto the porch and grabbed each boy under an arm. With apparent ease, he lifted them, placing one across each shoulder.

7. Unfriendly Assistance

"Looky here. I found me two sacks of taters," said the big man. As he walked towards Lauren, she saw the deer hide boots and pants beneath his cloak, which marked him as a frontiersman.

The boys flailed, knocking the man's hood off.

"Uncle!" Lauren called as she recognized Father's eldest brother. *Oh Lord, thank you! You've sent us help.*

"Coo Coo!" Ethan cried and laughed as Uncle bounced the boys up and down on his shoulders.

He set the boys down and turned back to his horse to tie off the reins to the hitching post.

All three children raced to give him a hug.

"That'll be enough of that now. Can't have you all thinking yer old uncle has gone all soft. Yer gran sent me down here to check on you all and yer ma after we heard your pa had gone missing."

"You know about Daddy?" Ethan asked.

"Yeah. Apparently, as soon as it happened, them not-so-Mighty Mercenaries sent out some messenger pigeons, and the local constable told us straight away."

Father and Knight Protector are Mighty Mercenaries; how dare he say it like that! Lauren knew Father was proud to work with the Mighty Mercenaries. They didn't all follow the Light, but Father said they helped people.

Uncle patted his saddle-laden Clydesdale, "I nearly rode these horses to death gettin' down here as fast as I could." The packhorse tied to the Clydesdale whinnied in unexpected agreement. This is a pretty big place for you all and yer ma to handle on yer own." Uncle scanned the barnyard. "Plus, I figured I might be able to help track yer pa down if I knew where to start. So . . . where's yer ma? I want to speak to her."

"She's gone. The Darkness has her." Ethan looked up at their uncle with sad puppy dog eyes.

Uncle dropped to one knee and stared intently at Ethan, "The *what* has her?"

"The Darkness." Lauren stepped up to put herself between the big man and her little brother. "She went looking for Daddy as soon as she heard he was missing."

Uncle's upraised eyebrow and frown made Lauren think he didn't believe what she was saying. She put her clenched fists on her hips. "That was almost a week ago. Ethan had a dream. Maybe vision is a better word. She's locked in a dark place, and she told him we should go to Blooming Glen."

Uncle grabbed Lauren by the shoulders and stared her down. "You mean to tell me yer ma finds out yer pa has gone missing, and she up and leaves you all on your own to tend this farm?"

The force of his presence sent a chill down Lauren's spine. All she could do was nod.

He stood up and looked around. "Did she get some help, at least? If she waited, I would have gone with her or, better yet, left her here with you all."

He looked down at the children with a furrowed brow. "I don't know much about this Darkness business, but I'll tell you going off into the wilderness on her own was no job for a woman."

"Hey! That's my mama you are talking about!" Aiden leaned forward with his hands balled into fists.

Uncle pointed his index finger at the boy. "Now listen here, I'm sure yer ma is good at teachin' you kids letters and numbers and how to do your chores, but findin' people lost in the wilderness is man's work."

Aiden took a step back and looked pleadingly at Lauren. Mama was good at teaching, but Father said she fought the Darkness before the kids were born. He was about to correct Uncle, but Uncle was on a roll, "So, who's helping you kids keep up the place while she's gone?"

Before Lauren could formulate an answer, Ethan piped up, "Well, no one, really. We got some help from Nicolas, but he died in the battle last night."

"The battle! What battle?" Uncle reached for the double-bitted axe on his saddle and pulled it free.

"The bishop came with the Hell dogs . . ." Aiden pointed towards the tower "and tried to take down the Light. We beat him with our weapons and Nicolas's help."

Aiden's hand fell to the sword, hilt at his waist, "But they killed him." Sorrow flowed over Lauren at the memory of Nicolas's sacrifice.

"Now, hold on! Are you telling me you kids fought a battle to keep Hell Hounds from taking down the light in the tower?" Uncle moved the axe to a two-handed grip. The way he was looking down at them made Lauren feel like they were on trial.

"Yep. Knight Protector told me to shine my light, and the bad dogs went poof!" Ethan pressed his fingers on both hands together and then spread them out to show the 'poof'.

"Poof, huh?" Uncle's eyes narrowed. "What knight protector?"

"Didn't you cross paths with him on the way here from town?" Aiden pointed up the road.

Uncle looked over his shoulder and paused. "I did just about get run off the trail by an oldster in armor goin' the other way." Uncle spat into the yard. "Them not-so-Mighty Mercenaries always think they're the most important people in the road."

This sent a chill through Lauren. *Was Uncle the type of person to start a fight over that kind of slight?* Knight

Protector would be back soon. She needed to calm things down before then.

Ethan broke in before Lauren could respond, "He was going back to town to make plans to take us to Blooming Glen, where there are a lot of knight protectors, and the light is safe. Just like my dream."

Oh no! Ethan, why couldn't you keep quiet? Lauren just knew they were sunk now.

"Well, I don't know about all this other stuff yer saying." Uncle reached into his cloak and pulled out a scroll with a seal on it. "But yer pa said that if anything ever happened to him and yer ma, you should come live with Gran in Fairfields."

We just had this conversation. Lauren let out a deep sigh. Uncle didn't seem to really be listening to them, so she didn't think she should bother until the knight protector returned. She took the scroll. It was identical to the one the bishop had shown her in the church.

"You kids should be with kin, not all locked up in some garrison somewhere." Uncle rested his axe on the ground, balanced by both hands holding the center of the bit. "That's what yer pa would want. Time's a-wasting; let's get on packing up."

Lauren turned her back to Uncle to show the boys the scroll with their father's seal. *We're in dangerous water with Uncle now.* She caught their eyes and put her finger to lips, and whispered, "Shhh."

The document was very official. It bothered her that the bishop had had the same instructions, but if their uncle brought it, then he must have gotten it directly from Father.

Grasping for a way to stall, she turned to Uncle, "Shouldn't we wait for the knight protector to come back? I think he was going to get supplies and stuff for the trip to Blooming Glen."

Uncle shook his head. "We don't need them not-so-Mighty Mercenaries in our business." He grabbed the axe below the head and hung it back on his saddle. "My horses can pull the wagon I see over there by the barn. It's big enough to supply us for the ten days it'll take us to get to Gran's."

Uncle untied his lead horse and turned to the children. "We can top off water and necessities at Loggerton. It's about halfway. I'll get the horses hitched, and we can start packin'." Uncle tugged on the lead horse's reins in the direction of the barn, and the packhorse followed.

He thinks he's on a mission, and there's no stopping him. Knight Protector said there would be consequences if we didn't listen to the 'still small voice.' What could they be if Uncle just packs us off to Grandma's?

She had to think of a way to stop him or even slow him down. "It's already past noon. Do you mean to have us travel tonight?" Surely Knight Protector would be back today.

"No, we'll get packed up today and head out at first light," Uncle responded over his shoulder.

Knight Protector said he'd return soon. Hopefully, he could help with Uncle. *Better to seem helpful than to start an argument.* "I'll go get the slate, and we can make a checklist like Mama has us do for chores."

Uncle merely waved his free hand dismissively in her direction while he guided the horses toward the wagon.

***

Lauren felt that she and the boys did a good job coming up with all the things they would need to take with them. The slate was three-quarters full when Uncle came into the kitchen.

Uncle looked over the slate. "That's a purty good list. You know how to make hardtack?"

This threw Lauren off a bit; she wasn't expecting Uncle to be complimentary. "Yes, sir."

He took the slate, added hardtack, and rattled off a half dozen items as he wrote. "There, that does it. Lauren, you get on that hardtack, and I'll get the boys helpin' me. Anything I'm missin'? Think about what your pa took the last time you visited Gran."

"Sparkle Frog." Ethan looked up at the big man with puppy-dog eyes.

Uncle raised an eyebrow. "Sparkle what?"

"Sparkle Frog," Ethan enunciated very carefully.

45

Aiden grabbed Uncle's work-weathered hand, "And Daddy Duck."

"Now, hold on. I'm sure your pa didn't bring no frog or no duck along on your last visit." Uncle caught Lauren's eye as if looking for help.

She glanced down at the slate and wrote for a second.

Uncle let out an exasperated huff, "Well, Lauren, you got a surprise to put on that list too?"

She turned the slate around where they could see, and the words "Meow Meow" were written at the bottom of the list with the O's in the shape of a pointy-eared cat head with two eyes, a nose, and whiskers in the middle. As if on cue, Meow Meow came out of the kitchen and started rubbing up against her leg.

"But, Uncle, they need us," Ethan put on his most pitiful pout.

Uncle pursed his lips, apparently mulling this over. "They need you, huh? If they need you, how are you fixin' to bring them along?"

"Meow Meow is pretty simple," Lauren said as she picked up her kitten and put him in her apron pocket, and smiled at Uncle.

"E, and I don't quite have that figured out yet." Aiden pointed to Uncle's head. "Daddy said you are super smart with animals, so we were kind of hoping you might be able to help us."

Ethan clasped his hands together, "Pweez, Coo Coo. Help me bring Sparkle Frog."

"All right then, the frog's not so hard." Uncle pointed out the front door towards the path to the creek. "Ethan, see that big rock over there by the edge of the path."

Ethan nodded, eyebrows raised.

"You go take that down by the frog's waterin' hole." Uncle took a knee and looked Ethan in the eyes. "You put that there rock in the sunniest spot you can find."

Lauren was surprised by this sudden turnaround. He seemed so gruff earlier, but now he was acting so sweet to Ethan. She wondered if she'd misjudged him.

"Before you know it, yer frog will be sacked out on it." Uncle grabbed a wooden bucket and lid from under the counter.

"Then pick up the rock real careful like and put it in this here bucket." He offered the bucket to Ethan.

"You're so smart, Coo Coo!" Ethan took the bucket and ran for the path.

Lauren's heart lightened at Ethan's enthusiasm. *This isn't going to be so bad. He's good with Ethan.*

Uncle looked at Aiden and rubbed his hand down his beard. "The duck's a whole other story. I've done my share of falconin', and getting a bird to stick around where you want it is no easy trick." Uncle stood up. "Aiden, help me get the supplies together. Then we'll tackle the duck problem. Not to worry about that kitten, either, Lauren. We'll take yer cow along, and the cat'll have cream every day."

We're all going to stay together. A wave of relief passed over her, and she smiled.

Uncle smiled back through his bushy beard, "Why don't you make us about four dozen hardtack biscuits?"

Lauren nodded enthusiastically. She enjoyed cooking, and if he wanted that many biscuits, the knight protector would surely be back before they were done. "OK, Uncle, I'll get on that right away."

Uncle turned to Aiden. "Come along, Aiden. Let's get that wagon loaded up."

"Yes, sir!" Aiden gave Uncle a smart salute, and they left the kitchen with a purpose.

Lauren set Meow Meow on the floor and began to gather the supplies for the hardtack. As her hands busied themselves with a familiar task, her mind wandered. Uncle had a writ just like the one the bishop showed her. If Father gave new ones to Knight Protector, what happened to the new instructions?

8. Mail Delivery

"Boy! Wake up!" The acolyte felt a hard shove in his chest as he opened his bleary eyes.

He woke in a room poorly lit by candle flames. The pressure on his shoulder was from a man who stood over him, shaking him awake. Something was off. His chest lay on a table, and he was seated on a rough wooden stool. As he took in his surroundings, he realized he was clothed in a yellow robe and had a quill pen in his hand.

Hadn't he passed out in the woods? How had he gotten here?

The armored man in front of him slapped his gauntleted hand on the table. "Scribe! Where's the Postmaster?"

The youth dropped the pen and rubbed his eyes. The room didn't come into any better view. Things were fleeting in and out of focus. The armored man was old but indistinct except for the symbol of the Mighty Mercenaries on the man's armor, denoting him as a knight protector. But that voice was so familiar.

Another dream.

The youth found himself saying, "He went to the privy, sir. How may I serve you?"

The man set two rolled pieces of parchment on the table. "I need to send a sealed message to the parsonages in Fairfields and the Heathlands." The knight took two leather dispatch tubes off the table next to him. He put a roll in each tube and latched them closed with the brass buckle and leather strap.

Fairfields? The Heathlands? Something about those places made the acolyte uneasy. His dreaming mind couldn't put it together.

He found himself saying, "We have our monthly words of faith messages going to both of those places on the morrow. On my honor, I will be sure your messages get there swiftly." But he didn't know why.

The acolyte watched the knight melt sealing wax over the buckle and pressed his seal into it.

"See to it that you do." The knight handed the two packages to the acolyte and turned to leave. As the warrior opened the tent, the acolyte noticed a large, brightly colored pavilion being erected in front of a chapel. He recognized the chapel; he was in Loggerton. But something was off; an odd haze seemed to have set in over the town.

He tried to focus on the scene outdoors as the knight protector exited. The tent flap dropped back into place and abruptly re-cast the scene in front of him into dim candlelight and continued to dim until his dreaming state was only blackness.

9. Duck Hunting

Aiden and Uncle worked diligently to prepare the wagon and supplies for their journey. Aiden was surprised at how patient Uncle was about showing him how to tie things down and pack things well.

When Ethan came back from the stream, Uncle gave him simple jobs that were just right for a little kid. Despite the growing connection with Uncle, Aiden worried about what would happen when the knight protector came back.

Ethan set a heavy wool blanket on the bed of the wagon for Aiden to stow. "Coo Coo, do you think the rock is hot yet?"

"I don't know. Guess we'd better go find out." Uncle placed Ethan on his shoulders and walked toward the woods, Ethan's giggles trailing behind them. Aiden smiled. He hadn't heard Ethan laugh like that since Daddy was home.

Before grief could overtake him, he hopped down from the wagon to go check on Lauren. The smell of warm biscuits hit him as he entered the kitchen. The scratching of a metal pan on the brick stove told him she was putting more biscuits into the oven.

He was about to ask her how he could help when he heard a horse and wagon approaching in the distance.

Lauren dusted her hands on her apron, and her head snapped towards the kitchen door. "Aiden, do you hear that?"

"Yeah, it could be Knight Protector. Let's go. We need to tell him about Uncle." Aiden rushed out of the kitchen, hoping to talk to Knight. Protector before Uncle got back from the stream.

The knight protector came into view on his horse with a black lacquered wagon drawn by two black horses following behind him. That wagon only came to funerals. It must be the mortician and the hearse coming to take Nicolas to be buried. Tears welled in Aiden's eyes at the thought of Nicolas's brave sacrifice. He snuffled it back and waited for them to come to the porch.

The knight dismounted. "What's all this?" he pointed to the loaded wagon," I didn't see these horses in your barn, and I appreciate the industry, but the arrangements are not all in place." Knight Protector began tying off his horse.

Aiden and Lauren shared a worried glance before Lauren started, "Our uncle came with a copy of the writ the bishop showed us."

Knight Protector stopped cold with the reins in his hand and turned big eyes to Lauren.

Lauran continued, "Uncle said he's going to take us to Grandma's house."

The elder warrior dropped the reins. "Your father's brother is here?" He scanned the yard. "Where is he?"

Aiden dashed over and scooped up the reins. "He's with Ethan at the creek right now, trying to catch Sparkle Frog."

Knight Protector put his hands on his hips and scanned the woods. "After our discussion this morning, do you think he's right to do this?"

Aiden was taken aback by this. He did agree that it seemed like the 'still small voice' was telling them to go to Blooming Glen. Knight Protector was a stranger, though, and Uncle was family.

"Well, he talked to Daddy and has his paper." The quiver in Aiden's voice gave away his uncertainty. "I don't know if he heard the small voice."

"I see." Knight Protector frowned. "And you, Lauren?"

"I believe Ethan's dream and your story about Daddy changing his mind. I'm worried about the consequences if we don't follow that." Lauren looked sympathetically at Aiden. "But without the writ you said you had, I don't think he'll believe you."

The hearse pulled to a stop next to them. Four workmen sat in the back of the black wagon. A fifth, the driver, a small man with black hair wearing a black-on-black suit, reached out with his riding crop and tapped the knight protector on his shoulder.

The elder warrior turned to him. "Gentlemen, I am sorry. You are waiting for me. Take the hearse to the base of the tower. The deceased is there. I will help you in just a moment." He took a thick key from his leather belt pouch and gave it to the driver, then returned his attention back to Aiden. "I didn't want you children to be scared by these men who've come to prepare Nicolas to be buried." Knight Protector took a knee and looked from Lauren to Aiden. "There will be a service first thing tomorrow morning."

Aiden frowned and snuffled up his tears. *Would he always be so sad? Would it hurt forever?*

Knight Protector patted Aiden on the head. "Unfortunately, I have other duties to attend to. Tomorrow we can finish preparations to go to Blooming Glen."

"What! You're leaving?" Aiden couldn't believe it. They needed to know what was going on. Were they really going to Blooming Glen, or would they go to Grandma's house first?

Before Aiden could object, Knight Protector said, "You should be safe enough. Your father told me your uncle is a formidable warrior."

Knight Protector stood.

Lauren grabbed his hand in both of hers, "Can't you just wait a few minutes for him to return, so we can work out where we're going?"

"There's a chance the new writ was just delayed, and even now, the parson has clear instructions from your father." Knight Protector patted her hand. "Your uncle has your father's word and a document backing that up."

He turned to Aiden. "If it's true that he can't hear the 'still small voice,' I'll need the help of the parson to convince him otherwise. Better to not start the dispute without the support."

Aiden knew Uncle could be stubborn. The knight protector was right that getting help would be better for that argument. Aiden nodded his agreement.

"Please ask him to bring you all to the early morning funeral, and then he and I can discuss the plan for ensuring your safety." Knight Protector mounted his horse and retrieved the key from the mortician before galloping off. The hearse followed at a measured pace.

Aiden turned to Lauren, "I've never been to a funeral before."

"Me either," Lauren looked down at her feet and shook her head, "but Nicolas saved us, and we should say goodbye."

Aiden knew how she felt. Losing Nicolas and Mama and Daddy was just too much. But these thoughts were overwhelmed by the question of where they were going. "Do you think Knight Protector will find the paper he's looking for?"

"I don't know, but it seems like Uncle is pretty determined to get us to Grandma's house. I don't know how Knight Protector is going to convince Uncle otherwise." She turned towards the kitchen, sniffing. "The biscuits!"

Lauren raced into the kitchen. Aiden was about to follow, but he heard Ethan giggling in the distance behind him. Uncle was coming back, so now they could get Daddy Duck. He wanted to ask Lauren what she thought the consequences might be if they went to the wrong place, but that would just have to wait. He wasn't going anywhere without Daddy Duck. Besides, maybe the knight protector was right, and the new paper was just late.

10. Return to Sender

A slight breeze sent a reflexive shiver through the unconscious youth. The action activated a hidden memory of the boy cowering on one knee before a powerful man in heavy blood-red robes.

The bishop!

The acolyte held up two messenger cases to the bishop. "Your Holiness! The Mercenaries send secret word to the parsons in Fairfields and the Heathlands."

The bishop took the offered cases. "Well done. These Mercenaries cannot be trusted; they know nothing of the true light." He motioned dismissively for the acolyte to be gone.

The acolyte stood, a deep knot in his stomach. Deep down, his instincts warned that the bishop was a man to be feared. The favor he just gained could be lost with the slightest mistake.

He opened the door to leave when the bishop called, "Wait, boy!"

Oh No! What did I do?

It took all his self-control to stop slamming the door closed. He turned slowly and dropped to one knee. "Yes, Your Holiness."

"No need for that." The bishop motioned for the youth to stand and pointed to the partially unrolled parchment on the table. "This is a great boon you just offered to me. You are truly destined for great things!"

Really? It was just a couple of letters. Should I ask?

"Come, come." The bishop waved the acolyte over to the table and spread out one of the documents. "The enemy has revealed his ultimate strategy."

The bishop traced a line of text. "See here? He believes that the tower he built in the Heathlands is secure."

He turned to a map behind him. "He thinks the power of a similar tower in Blooming Glen would have a doubling effect." He drew his finger down the map in a line from Blooming Glen to the Heathlands. "This would shine their unholy light through the center of our territory, separating our forces and preventing resupply from the North to the South."

The acolyte vaguely recalled many sermons on the battle for the true light. But he thought that was a metaphor. Laying it out on the map made the concept of a literal war very real.

"The fool," the bishop spat. "He believes his children have the power to defeat us."

"Our lord is the master of the Earth." The bishop placed his hands on the table and stared into the acolyte's eyes. "I see an unfortunate accident befalling this Mighty Mercenary and his family."

What does that mean? The Acolyte felt uneasy about where this was going.

The bishop came around the table and put an arm around the acolyte's shoulder. "Without him, his children will be easy enough to turn. But gaining access to the tower. That's something else."

Turning the children to the true light didn't sound like a bad thing, especially if their father was a heretic. But what's this about the tower?

The youth looked up to the elder cleric. "Your Holiness, just tell me what to do, and I'll do it."

"You and I are too close to the true light for this mission." The bishop shook his head. "Attempting to hold the lantern of the false light would sear our very souls. We need a lesser acolyte who has not yet bonded fully with the true light."

The acolyte's face fell at this. He hoped he could finally get a mission where he might be able to earn the Rose robes.

"Never fear," the bishop released the acolyte's shoulder and patted him on the back. "You will be my personal aid on our trip to the Heathlands. Be on your way now and send the most senior Violet Acolytes to see me. I must pick our traveling companion."

The acolyte left, and a wave of relief passed over him upon leaving the bishop's presence.

11.Blood is Thicker than Water

Uncle carried Ethan on his shoulders and his weather-worn right hand held a lidded wooden milk pail. Ethan waved at Aiden with his left hand while holding onto Uncle with his right, "Coo Coo is so smart. He told me to sit down next to the rock and just rub Sparkle Frog on the head gently between his eyes. Sparkle Frog really liked that, and then he just fell asleep."

Ethan rubbed Uncle's forehead for emphasis, and Uncle stopped walking and closed his eyes, and nodded off to one side to pantomime Ethan's story. Ethan continued, "Coo Coo just picked up the rock with Sparkle Frog on it and put him in the bucket!"

Uncle opened his eyes and raised the bucket in triumph.

"Wow, Uncle! Good job!" Aiden was happy for Ethan. Now it was his turn. "Do you have a trick for catching Daddy Duck?"

Uncle opened his mouth as if to reply, then stopped and scanned the yard warily. "Hey! Who's been here? There's fresh tracks all over."

Before Aiden could respond, Lauren stepped behind him and put a hand on his shoulder. "Knight Protector brought the mortician for Nicolas."

Uncle put the bucket and Ethan down. "That high and mighty mercenary came back, and you didn't come to get me?" His face was turning red.

Aiden didn't like how Uncle's eyebrows were furrowed. A knot formed in his stomach, "He was just here for a few min—"

"Look here! Till yer ma and pa come back, or we get to Grandma, I'm yer guardian." He pointed at them with his index finger, then back at himself with his thumb. "That means it's my job to guard you!"

The knot in Aiden's stomach tightened. *Uncle was mad. Would he give them a spanking? Or worse?* Ethan must have been feeling the same way as he ran over and hid behind Aiden.

Uncle pointed back at his chest again. "Me and nobody else. I don't want you talkin' to anybody 'cept me unless I'm there."

He pointed up the road, "Especially if them high and mighty mercenaries come back. It's them, and their nonsense got yer pa in trouble in the first place."

That wasn't right, and Aiden knew it. But he was too afraid to say anything under Uncle's imposing glare.

Uncle put his fists on his hips. "Next time someone shows up, you come get me, no exceptions! You all got that?"

"Yes, sir." Aiden heard his siblings say in unison with his reply. He didn't like this at all. He trusted Knight Protector and the parson. Uncle shouldn't keep them from talking to the kids.

Uncle exhaled, and the red in his face started to recede. "So, what did his high and mightiness want?"

Aiden looked up over his left shoulder at Lauren. She nodded at him, so Aiden explained, "He just came to take Nicolas to get him ready for the funeral first thing tomorrow morning."

Ethan began to cry, which brought some tears to Aiden's eyes as well.

"Oh now, there's no need for all that," Uncle came forward with a handkerchief. "This Nicolas was a friend of yours?"

Aiden wiped his eyes on his sleeve and turned to Ethan, who was crying in earnest. Uncle took a knee and wiped Ethan's eyes. "Losin' people's tough stuff. But sayin' goodbyes proper makes it a bit easier. We'll go to the funeral."

Aiden was surprised by the turnaround. It seemed like Uncle could get super mad out of nowhere and then suddenly turn all nice. He was hard to figure out. *Which would it be when Knight Protector challenged him on where to take them?*

As if he were reading Aiden's mind, Uncle said, "So what else did he have to say? Any more about this Blooming Glen nonsense?"

Lauren stepped in. "He said that was a discussion that you and he should have tomorrow."

Aiden thought that was a clever answer. He would have been tempted to lie despite how it would dim the tower, but Lauren's answer was perfectly true.

Uncle stood back up, "Well, I guess I'll let him say his piece and be done with it."

The tension in Aiden's stomach eased. Still, he was worried. *What if they didn't do what they should? Consequences.*

Uncle turned to him and locked eyes. "You still thinkin' we'll be takin' a duck with us?"

Aiden nodded enthusiastically.

Ethan sniffed. "I want to help!"

Aiden wasn't sure that was a good idea. He was about to object, then thought better of it. *Ethan couldn't make catching Daddy Duck any harder, could he?*

***

Uncle led the boys over to his horse.

"Alrighty, putin' a frog in a bucket is one thing. Bringin' that duck along is somethin' else. We don't have a proper cage, so I'm not sure I've got a good way to do this. The duck's too big for a bucket, plus it's likely to hurt itself." Uncle looked off in the distance thoughtfully.

Aiden thought about it too. What could he find to keep Daddy Duck caged? Then he remembered a story Father told him. "Daddy said you were a really top-notch falconer. Could you teach me for Daddy Duck?"

"Training a falcon is a long process that takes a lot of equipment and care." Uncle paused and rubbed his hand down his beard. "I've never heard of anybody trying to train a duck. The falcon's a solitary predator. Ducks are flocking birds." Uncle pursed his lips and shook his head. "The instincts are all wrong; don't think it'd take to the training."

It seemed like Uncle might be giving up before they got started. Aiden wasn't going to let that happen. "Do we need to 'train' Daddy Duck? I was just thinking about the falcon stuff—the hood, and the glove and string and stuff."

"Oh, well now, that could be interesting." Uncle began digging around in his saddlebags. "The problem is that if the cage isn't the right size, the blindfolded bird will beat its wings on the sides and damage its feathers."

Uncle pulled out various leather odds and ends and set them on the horse's back. "If we're going to put your duck in a box, we need to figure out a way to keep it calm."

He held up a dome-shaped piece of black leather with two big round bumps evenly spaced near the top of the dome and two strings hanging from the bottom, "Putting a falcon hood on it might do just the trick." Uncle handed the falcon hood to Aiden. "If you can figure out how to get this on the duck, that should calm it enough for us to transport it in just about anything."

Aiden took the hood in both hands and tried to see if it would stretch out any bigger. Uncle must have been thinking the same thing as Aiden when he said, "It's made for a falcon's head, so I don't know that it will fit on your duck. We may have to turn it sideways or backward and figure out a different way to strap it on, but it should work." Uncle pulled a brown woven cord about an eighth of an inch thick out of his bag. "This here cord will help keep it from flyin' off once we catch it."

"This is a great idea, Uncle!" Aiden ran off toward the pond and called back over his shoulder, "Let's go catch him."

"Alright, I'm coming." Uncle tied the saddlebag closed. "Ethan, you better come along too. That frog of yours is going to need some food on this trip." Uncle pointed towards the foxtails on the side of the pond. "I'm bettin' there's plenty of grasshoppers and bugs that you can catch to put in the bucket."

"Good idea, Coo Coo," Ethan ran towards where Uncle was pointing.

***

Lauren was a bit jealous as she realized the boys were off on an adventure. She was glad Uncle was letting them take the animals. Each one had helped them defeat the Darkness in their own special way. Even leaving one behind might leave them vulnerable. But if she was being honest, tending the biscuits was no grand adventure.

"The biscuits!" she ran into the kitchen and pulled them out of the oven quickly. She was in such a hurry that she didn't have a good hold of the hot pads as she pulled the tray out, and it burned her fingers.

She powered through the pain long enough to set it on the pinewood counter. Then she quickly pulled her hands away and put her fingers in the pail of water they kept by the fire. This cooled the pain in her fingertips. She pulled her hands out of the water and looked at them. They were a little pink but not actually blistered. It wasn't the first time she had burned herself—or the worst—so she shrugged it off and turned back to the biscuits.

She looked around the kitchen for the spatula and realized that Ethan had taken it out with the supplies they were packing. She found a wooden fork and used that to pry one of the biscuits off the sheet. The fork wasn't ideal as it broke up the biscuit instead of separating it cleanly from the sheet. The biscuit was only dark brown on the bottom, so she was satisfied she hadn't burnt them. She decided it would be better to use the right tool for the job and went out to retrieve the spatula.

As she stepped outside, a splash from the pond caught her attention. She ran to find out what was happening and rounded the corner of the house just in time to see Daddy Duck taking to the air with a "Quack!" As she drew near to the pond, Ethan scrambled out of the pond, soaked head to toe and sputtering water.

Aiden shouted, "Awww, man!"

Lauren could tell by his tone; he was frustrated with Ethan. However, Aiden's cry must have sounded different to Daddy Duck. The duck glided in and, with a gentle flap of its wings, landed on Aiden's head. Uncle was standing right beside Aiden and used this as the opportunity to grab the duck by the neck.

Daddy Duck squawked and flapped his wings. Uncle stepped closer and forced the duck's wings down, and tucked the bird's struggling body under his arm. Uncle pulled Daddy Duck's head down to a level Aiden could reach, and then Aiden put the hawk hood on it.

Instantly, Daddy Duck stopped struggling. Uncle seemed so gruff and even mean sometimes. But it was comforting to watch him firmly but securely hold Daddy Duck while he talked Aiden through securing the hood on the bird's head.

A sloshing noise made Lauren turn to see Ethan approaching from the pond. He looked like a drowned rat. Before she could get on him about it, Aiden ran over and hugged him. "Thanks, E! You helped catch Daddy Duck!"

Aiden stepped back, and Lauren saw that his clothes were also a soaked mess. *What am I going to do with those boys?*

Ethan frowned. "I lost all my bugs."

Aiden patted Ethan on the shoulder and looked up. "Uncle, do you have Daddy Duck? I want to help E get some more bugs."

Uncle's smile was more noticeable in the creases in his eyes than through his bushy beard. "Yeah, I suppose." He tucked the duck deeper under his arm and started walking toward the barn.

Lauren took this as her cue to return to her task. She was glad to see Uncle and the boys getting along so well. She picked up the cast-iron spatula from the wagon on her way to the kitchen. After removing all the nearly burned biscuits from the tray, she cleaned it off and oiled it before putting the last batch into the oven.

With all the activity, Lauren almost missed that it was already dinner time, and she was hungry. She was sure it would only be a few minutes before the boys would come complaining of the same thing. She looked around the kitchen and began scrounging the last bits of things to make a "must-go" meal because everything must go, or it will be left to rot.

But where must we go? The choice seemed clear to her: Blooming Glen. Uncle sounded like he was dead set otherwise. What were the consequences of not following the 'still small voice'? She really didn't want to end up in the dark belly of a fish.

12.Obey Your Elders

Uncle and the boys came in just as Lauren was finishing dinner.

"You know, I was just thinkin' it was time fer some chow. Yer ma really taught you right, Lauren." Uncle sniffed the air. "Mmmm, good! Supper ready when it's time and cookin' with bacon grease. Don't get much better than that."

"Thank you, Uncle." Lauren blushed and gave a little curtsy. *Uncle really can be sweet when he wants to be.*

When they were all seated, Uncle put both his hands on the table. "Before we get to eatin', we need to talk about tomorrow. That way, I know I've got yer full attention."

Oh No! He really doesn't understand little boys. Lauren glanced at Ethan, wondering how long it would take for him to start whining because he was hungry.

Uncle said, "If it's a proper sunrise service to put yer friend to rest, then they're goin' to have a wake afterward." His eyes darted between the three of them, intent on keeping their attention. "Now, I don't know if you all have been to a funeral before, but it's a pretty somber occasion. You all need to be in yer best clothes and on yer best behavior."

Lauren found herself reflexively saying, "Yes, sir," with the boys. Father had had a few of these talks around the table *after* dinner.

"Afterward, me and this knight protector of yours will have a talk if that's what he wants." Uncle's tone made Lauren think his mind was made up already. Uncle stood up. "Now, I don't know anything about this knight protector, and it seems his kind got yer pa and ma into a mess of trouble." He slapped his hand sharply on the table for emphasis.

The children jumped back in their seats. Lauren looked at Ethan and could tell by his wide eyes he was scared. She looked back to Uncle, and he continued, "If yer parents raised you right, and I know they did based on how good of workers you were today, then you know blood is thicker than water. Right?"

Blood, water, what? Lauren felt he had completely lost it. She looked to the boys, who shrugged. She did likewise. "Um … I guess that's right, but it's just gross."

Uncle did a double take. "Never mind that. What I'm saying is, family is the most important thing."

"Oh, I get it." Aiden raised his hand like he was in Sunday school. "Blood, like blood relations. But what's the water?"

"The water . . . it's a sayin': blood is thicker 'n' water." Uncle looked around the room for a minute like he was trying to find some example.

He shook his head, "We're kin, you see, and kin's got to stick together. So, you all need to stick with me, got it?" He put his hands on his hips. "I don't know what yer knight protector's plannin', but I do know yer gran would

71

never forgive me if I let anything happen to you, nibbles."
He pointed at each of the children for emphasis and then
back at himself. "So, you need to follow my lead regardless
of what kind of story the knight protector might be telling."

"OK, Coo Coo." Ethan looked at Aiden, then Lauren.
"We don't want Grandma to be mad at him, right?"

Lauren pursed her lips and nodded as she looked at
Aiden out of the corner of her eye to gauge his reaction. He
nodded as well. She understood what Uncle was saying, but
she knew that Knight Protector had their best interests at
heart.

Uncle grabbed his fork, "That's settled then. Let's eat."

***

After dinner, Uncle went to tend the horses, and the
children worked together to clean up. As Lauren washed
the dishes, Aiden took a dish to dry and asked, "So what
are we really going to do?"

Lauren paused in washing. "I don't know for sure.
Uncle is right about family sticking together."

Aiden handed a plate to Ethan to put away. "But what
about the small voice? Shouldn't we listen to Ethan's dream
and go shine the Light like Mama said?"

Ethan pulled on Lauren's apron, "Coo Coo said he
wanted to make sure nothing bad happened to us. Can't he
come to help us light the tower?"

Lauren patted him on the top of his head. "I hope that is how it will work out."

Lauren had little confidence that Uncle would cooperate with Knight Protector. *He's just so stubborn.*

***

The children worked late into the evening, getting everything in order. Finally, they sat down with the Good Book, and Lauren read the verses for the day, which included:

"Children obey your elders …"

Uncle was apparently paying attention, "Yah, that's what I was sayin' earlier. We're kin, and I'm yer elder, so you all should be followin' my lead."

"Can you pray for us, Coo Coo?" Ethan folded his hands and looked up at his uncle.

Lauren focused on Uncle, intent on his reaction. *Will he pray with us? I sure hope so.*

Uncle seemed to squirm in his seat for a moment. "Ummm. You know that was something yer pa was always more interested in than I was. Not sure what you all should be prayin'," replied Uncle with a little pink showing on his cheeks above his fuzzy beard.

"Oh, I can teach you, Coo Coo." Ethan reached up and put his uncle's hands together, then clasped his own as well. "God bless Daddy. God bless Mommy. God bless, Lauren. God bless Aiden. God bless Ethan. God bless Papa.

73

God bless Grandma. God bless Uncle, and God, please keep the monsters, dragons, and The Dark One away."

"Amen!" the three children completed in unison.

Uncle patted Ethan on the head. "That's a good one. Now you all go to bed. We'll be up before you know it."

Lauren gathered the boys and directed them toward the ladder to the loft. She knew God was with them, but she wasn't sure about Uncle. Would he let them follow the 'still small voice' wherever it called?

13. The Stalker

The sound of hoofbeats, muted by damp dirt and the creak of a horse-drawn wagon, woke the teenage boy from the chaotic dreams that haunted him throughout the night. Wet morning dew soaked him, and a shiver went through his hunger-wracked body. The colors of day broke in the east. But he was confused by the light shining to his right.

He sat up with a groan as hunger cramped his stomach. His forehead didn't hurt anymore. He stilled himself for a moment to figure out where the wagon was coming from. A deep breath cleared his head and helped him identify that the sounds came from the top of the hill to his right. Would it be help or an enemy?

Hunger overcame any worry about an enemy, and he scrambled up the slope on all fours. At the top, he peeked over the hill to observe the wagon approaching, hoping the weeds on the roadside obscured him from view.

The little red-headed boy and his shield! It wasn't a concussion-addled dream. The evil little boy was real! There was his shield strapped to the side of the wagon, along with a sword and a spear! *The spear girl, I hate her. She did this to me!* The other boy from his dream was there too. They had a giant of a man driving their wagon.

Evil is upon me! His knees went weak, and he slid down the hill, with his heart racing a thousand miles an hour. He waited for his heart to slow down and the sound of the hoof beats to recede. He wanted to know where they went, but he couldn't see much from the bottom of the hill. Despite his reservations, he clamored up the hill as stealthily as he could.

He scanned the road in the direction the wagon had come from. The path that way appeared rarely traveled, and some vague memory told him it led to the evil children's home. *They're gone, but what traps or evil beings might be there to protect the tower?*

He turned in the direction the wagon traveled and saw the road would take the wagon towards a big white building with a tall, pointed tower at the front of it. There appeared to be a group of people gathering there. *That building, it's a ... what's the word ... church? A place of The Light? Right? Maybe they can help.* If he could get there, they would surely help him in his wretched state.

I need to warn them about the evil children! He surveyed the land between him and the church. The road curved out of view but appeared to wind back at a bridge. The wagon hadn't made it there yet. *If I'm careful, I can cut across the creek here and beat the wagon.*

He worked his way down the hill slowly to avoid slipping in the dew-soaked grass. Then he rushed to the creek bed and paused to drink his fill before jumping across the creek to the other side. He landed poorly and fell. His knee banged against a rock, and he let out a cry.

He looked around in all directions while his stomach did backflips. *Did they hear?* He hastily crawled under some bushes nearby and waited for the sound of footfalls or voices, rubbing his knee.

After five minutes of listening to the stream gurgling and other forest noises, his hunger outweighed his fear. *Am I too late to beat the wagon to the church?* He stood and found a hidden reservoir of energy that propelled him toward the church.

When he reached the field of tall grass near the church, he stopped and took a knee. *Too late!* The wagon carrying the evil kids had stopped at the gathering there.

If they are accepting of the evil children, has the whole church turned to The Darkness? The knot of anxiety growing in his stomach was quickly overshadowed by a deep rumbling and a wave of wooziness that hit him as he caught his breath.

He looked the church over and saw a cellar door at the rear of the building. *Maybe there's food in the basement.* The gathering seemed to be moving away from the church. If he could avoid whatever was going on in the front, he could sneak inside.

He crouched down and began to wade through the tall grass, careful to keep his head below the top of the grass to maintain concealment. When he reached the edge of the tall grass, he carefully peeked out to see what was going on with the people.

On the edge of the crowd, he thought he could make out the evil little girl. Her back was to him, but he was pretty sure it was her, and she was intently listening to a man in white who must be their leader. *The whole place is corrupt. I'm in no shape to fight. She might hurt me again. I must get in and out quickly so no one will notice.*

He steeled himself to run to the cellar doors, then dashed for the stone steps leading to the basement. He ran to the bottom and crouched before attempting to open the door. Luckily, it was not locked.

Cool, musty air chilled him. He crept inside and silently closed the door behind him. The basement's only light filtered from a crack under a door that led up to the church.

The floor was made of irregular limestones with mortar in between that matched the basement walls. An oil lampstand was fastened on the wall at the bottom of the stairs. He carefully walked towards it, trying to ensure he did not trip on anything.

A box of matches sat underneath the lamp holder. He lit the lamp, and his heart fell when he saw that the cellar was essentially empty. *No! I'm done for.* His breath came in short raspy gasps, and he swooned.

He fell to a knee and forced himself to breathe slowly through his nose. *By the red light! I will find something to eat!* He stood and began to search the darkened corners of the basement more carefully. Finally, he found some small bags of grain stacked in one corner. He couldn't decide what was worse, no food or food he had no way to prepare.

Maybe there was something *upstairs.* But could he sneak up there undetected? His stomach told him there was

78

only one way to find out, and his stomach told him he needed to do it now.

As dawn fully broke, the wagon approached the gathering on the hill. A crowd was gathered in their Sunday best at the newly dug grave in the cemetery beside the church. Uncle pulled the wagon up by picnic tables laid out for the wake and helped the children out. Ethan grabbed his uncle's work-worn right hand and looked up at him with tears pooling in his eyes.

"It'll be alright," Uncle's voice was the softest Ethan had ever heard it. Holding Uncle's hand, he walked in silence toward the graveyard. As they approached, the knight protector waved for them to come to the front of the gathering. Next to the freshly dug grave was a simple pine casket. Ethan's eyes went wide at the sight of Nicolas in the full armor of a knight protector. It was polished so well that it reflected the morning sunlight, making Nicolas look as if he were an angel coming down from heaven.

The transformation from the broken boy Ethan had last seen to the brilliant young man in the casket was too much for Ethan, and he began to weep in earnest. Lauren and Aiden were also overcome with grief. Uncle and Knight Protector both took a knee to let the children hug them and cry for what felt like an eternity.

The parson came up and patted Ethan on his head. Ethan looked up, and the man's familiar, tender smile warmed his heart. As Parson continued to the front of the congregation, Uncle pulled a paisley handkerchief from his pocket and helped Ethan wipe his tear-filled eyes. Then Uncle stood up and held onto Ethan's hand.

"Brothers and sisters, we are gathered here today to pay our respects to Sir Nicolas the Selfless." Parson began in a powerful tone that lifted Ethan's heart. *Nicolas was so brave!*

Apparently, the crowd had been told of his courage, and murmurs of ascent went through the crowd.

Parson continued, "He represents the very best of humanity. As the Good Book says, 'There is no greater love than to lay down one's life for another.'"

Ethan wanted to shout and tell everyone about his friend Nicolas. How the bad dogs were so scary, and he fought them for Ethan and his siblings. But Uncle's firm hand on his own and the somber crowd helped Ethan hold his tongue.

"This young man, still really a boy himself, paid the ultimate price so that the Tower of Light might still shine in these lands." Parson pointed towards the children's farm and the tower shining there. The crowd turned to look while Parson paused. "It is only fitting he be honored as a knight protector in death as he conducted himself as one in life." Ethan found himself nodding at this. Nicolas was a brave knight protector, just like Daddy.

The parson reached a hand toward Nicolas, "This young man was not a part of our community, but he gave his life for us as if he were. I ask if anyone has a word to say for Sir Nicolas, you may step forward and do so."

Immediately Ethan let go of Uncle's hand and ran forward. Then he turned to face the crowd.

"E!" Aiden started towards his brother, but Knight Protector put a hand on his shoulder.

Ethan took that as a sign it was OK to talk. "I can tell you about Nicolas."

The parson stepped to Ethan's side and slowly knelt on one knee. "Please, young Ethan, tell us about Sir Nicolas."

Ethan looked at the crowd and paused for a moment, not sure where to begin. Then he pointed toward their home. "Nicolas saved Sparkle Frog from the black water." Then he pointed at his siblings. "Then, he saved Sissy and Aiden from the bad dogs."

Ethan turned to Parson with a pleading look in his eyes. "He was my friend, and I miss him. Parson, please pray, and God will make him all better."

Parson's face fell at this request, leaving a lump in Ethan's stomach.

Ethan pleaded with his hands clasped together. "I prayed, and that wasn't good enough. You pray, and he will be all better."

"Oh, child," the pastor pulled Ethan to him in a kind embrace. "I am so sorry. I know you and your brother and sister have prayed much over Nicolas." Ethan began to sob into Parson's shirt. The parson stroked Ethan's hair. "God has him home in heaven now to watch over us. His mission here on Earth is done, and he is now free of all the conflict and pain that still visits these lands."

This made Ethan cry louder, and the crowd began to weep with him.

As Ethan's wail became a sob, Parson stood up. Ethan ran back to Lauren and Aiden, and the three of them embraced, lost in their sadness.

Parson wiped his own eyes with a white handkerchief, "Let us bow our heads in reverence to the Lord Almighty. Father God, we commit our brother Nicolas to you. We pray that if we are called to the aid of others, we will have the strength to follow the example of Sir Nicolas the Selfless. Amen."

The first row of parishioners walked past the casket, dropping strands of ivy into it. The others followed suit and then walked toward the church. When all the others had left, Uncle led the children to do the same, and Knight Protector followed.

The group gathered at a set of tables and benches in front of the church, set with eggs, meats, cheeses, and sweetbreads. When everyone found a seat on the rough wooden benches, Parson said a brief grace, and a somber meal ensued.

As Ethan handed a basket of biscuits to Aiden, he thought he saw someone dart from the tall grass behind the church to the doorway to the church cellar at the back of the church. *Is that a sneaky spy?*

"E, butter!" Aiden poked Ethan's shoulder.

Aiden's request distracted Ethan. "Manners!" Ethan snapped back.

"Butter, please!" Aiden barked. "I'm really hungry."

"Fine!" Ethan passed the butter and turned back to get a better look. He didn't see anything out of the ordinary. *Maybe it was nothing.*

A plate of sweet rolls was set next to him, and all thoughts of a spy running around vanished. He was hungry, just like Aiden. *I'll tell the parson about it later; now it's time to eat.*

15. Unexpected Excitement

Lauren took a sip of milk and remembered Meow Meow, who was still in the wagon. *Poor Kitty, he must be hungry.*

She looked to Parson at the head of the table, "Excuse me, Parson, sir. May I please be excused a moment to feed my kitten?"

"Why, yes, dear. That would be a fine thing to do. No need for your kitten to go hungry with this bounty here." The parson smiled.

She looked to Uncle just to be sure, and he gave her a curt nod. Lauren let out a sigh. She didn't realize how tense she was today. The funeral had wrung every bit of sorrow from her. Other worries made her tense too. Would Uncle listen to Knight Protector? Her stomach clenched at the thought of a confrontation between the two of them.

She felt a tug on her arm and looked down to see Ethan's expectant face looking up. "Oh, me too! Sparkle Frog needs food."

He scanned around as if looking for something important. "Oh wait, I don't see any bugs."

"We can take care of the bugs later." Uncle took a cinnamon roll off a plate. "There are lots of grasshoppers about. If yer quick, you can pull them right out of the air."

"Oh, I'm quick." Ethan beamed. It warmed Lauren's heart to see some of his normal enthusiasm return after the pain of the funeral.

Lauren turned to Aiden. "How about Daddy Duck?"

Aiden finished licking cinnamon roll icing from his fingers. "I think Daddy Duck will be fine. I gave him some worms before we left."

It seemed like Aiden was recovering well also, although it was always hard to tell with him. She'd have to talk to him later when others weren't around to be sure to get the truth of how he was doing.

Lauren excused herself and took a shallow bowl of milk with her to the wagon. *Careful now, don't spill it all.* She was glad it was only a few feet from the table, so she didn't have to walk far.

She found Meow Meow in the front of the wagon, trying to jump up on the seat. He had managed to get his claws stuck on the top edge of the board for the seat but could not pull himself up. His feet were pinwheeling in the air. *Poor kitty, hanging like that's got to hurt.* Lauren set the saucer of milk on the driver's seat and reached into the back of the wagon to grab the kitten.

This startled Meow Meow, and he clawed Lauren with his back paws.

"Ouch! Bad kitty!" She pulled her hand back quickly, then sucked on her clawed finger, bumping Sparkle Frog's bucket and knocking it onto its side. *Oh, no! If that frog gets out, there will be big trouble!* The last thing they needed was an animal hijinks at the funeral.

She scrambled up the steps to the driver's seat and was able to see that the lid was still securely on the bucket. Tension fled her muscles as she heard, "meow, meow."

You are so pitiful. Lauren reached down to pick up Meow Meow, convinced that disaster had been averted by the sturdy bucket lid. She let out a long breath as she gently pet Meow Meow's back. She was shaken out of her reverie by a thumping noise behind her, followed by the sound of trickling water.

She turned in time to see the bucket lid hit the wagon bed and Sparkle Frog hop out of the bucket. He announced his release from captivity with a big "Croak!"

Oh no! How was she going to get the frog back in the bucket without making a scene? She looked towards the crowd at the picnic tables, and no one seemed the wiser.

If I get him quick, no one will notice. She dropped the kitten and scrambled over the wagon seat. When she leaped at the frog, the playful amphibian jumped away, and she face-planted into a sack of grain. *Please, God, let me catch him before there's a scene.*

She looked up and saw Sparkle Frog sitting on a small barrel, staring down at her with his head cocked to one side. "Croak!" *He thinks I'm playing with him, like Ethan.*

Lauren got up very slowly, hoping not to startle the frog. She carefully slid her feet forward, keeping her eyes on the frog. Just a little closer. When she was in striking distance, she readied herself to pounce on the frog.

"Hey, Sissy! Watcha doin'?" Ethan called up from the side of the wagon. She reflexively turned towards his voice and lost sight of the frog.

"Ethan! No!" Too late. The morning sun perfectly reflected a rainbow streak through the air as Sparkle Frog jumped from the barrel onto Ethan's head. He let out a giggle and looked up cross-eyed at the frog.

Lauren turned toward the picnic tables and saw all eyes were turned to them. *We're in so much trouble.* Lauren's face flushed as she scanned around in the vain hope of finding a place to hide. But nothing stood out more than the sparkling frog on Ethan's redhead.

"E! What are you doing?" Aiden hopped up from his seat at the table.

"It wasn't it me!" Ethan was gradually raising his hands toward the frog.

Maybe he can get Sparkle Frog before it gets worse. Lauren held her breath.

Then Ethan slowly pointed his index finger in her direction. "Sissy was playing chase first."

That little rat! Lauren's jaw set. She was going to take care of this and give him a lesson about tattling. Before she could take a step, Ethan slapped his hands together to catch his pet. He moved a fraction of a second too late, and the frog jumped into the middle of a picnic table.

This elicited a mix of shrieks and harumphs of "Well, I've never" from the churchgoers. Aiden leapt onto the table after the frog.

Aiden, not you too. The heat in Lauren's face and the tension in her jaw was suddenly overshadowed by a deep sinking feeling in her stomach. *We're gonna get it!*

Aiden only managed to to scare the frog off the table and toward the tall grass on the edge of the churchyard— not to mention that he landed with one hand in a bowl of fresh strawberries and the other in a pound cake.

Aiden looked over his shoulder at Lauren as the color in his face began to match the strawberries. *Oh, Aiden, you're such a mess! What is Uncle going to do?*

Uncle laughed deeply with a wide grin you could see through his bushy beard. This caused the other grown-ups to look at him. "Next time you want the strawberry shortcake, just say, 'please pass.' You don't have to dive into it, boy."

Uncle's laugh caused Lauren to really look at the scene in front of her. Aiden was sticky with red strawberry juice oozing down his hands in the middle of the church breakfast, and Ethan's red curls were bouncing as he chased his frog. It was just about the funniest thing she had ever seen. All the tension left Lauren in an uncontrollable laugh.

Parson chuckled. "I know I've often been tempted to leap for the missus's strawberry shortcake myself, but your uncle is right."

That caused the rest of the table to break up laughing.

Aiden got up on his knees and looked at his messy hands, "But—but I wasn't trying to get cake." He looked pleadingly at Lauren. "I was trying to catch Sparkle Frog."

That only made Lauren laugh harder. *Poor Aiden.* She knew he was mortified, but she just couldn't help herself.

"Oh, is that what you were doin'?" Uncle said with a wink. "Well, it looks like he got away. You'd best be after him before one of these other youngsters gets him."

Uncle looked around the table. "I've got a bag of saltwater taffy fer, the one that gets the frog back in his bucket."

Aiden leaped off the table and followed Sparkle Frog. The handful of other children at the tables took off in a mad dash.

That was the last thing Lauren expected from Uncle. *Maybe everything will turn out alright.*

Lauren saw Uncle turn to look at Parson and Knight Protector. "We got things to talk about. That frog will keep them busy for a while. Let's step into yer office, Parson, and the three of us have a chat." It was like Uncle was reading her mind.

"Agreed," said Parson and Knight in unison. They excused themselves from the table, and Parson led them into the chapel.

Lauren's eyes followed the three men as they went inside. *Uncle's not so bad; maybe he'll take us to Blooming Glen like Daddy said, or maybe there will be consequences.*

16. The Confrontation

Acolyte's hunger finally overcame his fear, and he decided to sneak upstairs. He looked back at the lamp he'd lit. *I'll bring anything I find to eat back down here.* When he got to the top of the steps, he listened carefully at the door and didn't hear anyone, so he slowly opened it.

He stepped onto a landing in a small room. To his left, he discovered a wall with tall double doors without any ornaments or handles. They looked like they could be opened in either direction. Behind him, he found three stairs going up to a stage with a pulpit.

Directly in front of him stood a long counter containing all the articles used in a church service. This included two hard loaves of communion bread on a gold plate. He rushed to the platter and tore into the bread with abandon. *Mmmm, so good.*

He was so hungry he ate half the loaf before he realized he didn't have anything to drink. He spotted a half-full crystal decanter of red liquid on the counter with an ornate gold goblet next to it. He had a sudden aversion to it that he couldn't quite remember. It was something about it being for adults, but he couldn't remember exactly why.

He filled the goblet halfway and picked it up in both hands to drink. It didn't smell right. He couldn't place it, but his instincts told him it wasn't good. However, his thirst overcame him, so he decided to choke it down.

The liquid zapped his tongue with its sharp taste, but it had a sweetness to it. It smoldered in his stomach at first, and he wondered if it might make him throw up. He picked up some bread and ate it to take the edge off.

After a few minutes, the smoldering in his stomach subsided, and warmth crept up his cheeks. He decided quenching his thirst was worth enduring the sting of the drink and sat for a while, just munching the bread and sipping the red liquid. He finished the goblet and poured another one.

After a second glass, he started to feel funny. His head felt a little off, not dizzy, just off. Perhaps this was from two days without food. *What else could it be?* A slight creaking announced the sanctuary opening.

He froze in place, and the fear of being caught cleared his head momentarily. As he was trying to decide if he should run back downstairs, he heard voices.

"Look here, Mr. High and Mighty Mercenary," a deep, gruff voice declared, "those kids are my kin, and yer not taking them ANYWHERE without me!"

"I don't dispute your role in protecting the children," a more refined voice replied. "You are welcome to accompany the children and me to Blooming Glen to ensure their safety."

This sounds serious. Maybe they are talking about locking up those evil kids. The acolyte snuck up the stairs to the stage and carefully peeked around the corner.

93

He was greeted by the sight of a large man in frontiersman leathers with a bushy beard and hair. *It's the man from the wagon with the evil kids!* He was facing an old man in battered armor. He seemed very familiar, like from a dream, but the acolyte just wasn't sure. A third man was there, dressed in simple white clothes. He was the one that seemed to oversee the group outside the church earlier.

"Now listen here. Them kids ain't goin' to no Blooming Glen." The frontiersman pulled out a small scroll with seals on it and held it up. "They're going to Fairfields just like their pa said."

Realizing he was well hidden, fear abated. The acolyte continued to watch. However, his head felt like it was getting warmer, and his vision seemed to be closing in around the edges.

"I see," said the armored man as he took the scroll and reviewed it. "This was six months ago. I spoke to your brother three weeks ago."

He rolled up the scroll and handed it back to the frontiersman. "He gave me copies of new instructions that I put in the post myself in Loggerton. They were sent to your mother and the parson here."

The dream! This was the armored man from my dream. I took the instructions.

"While I'm sure that could be true, and no knight protector would fabricate such a tale," the parson paused for a moment as if sizing up the elderly warrior. "I have to say that I do not recall receiving a new writ. As you know,

I have been 'indisposed' these last few days. I will check my office and return with what I have."

The man in white moved off to the opposite side of the church from the acolyte, who crept down the stairs to avoid discovery. He listened intently for what might happen next. *What will he find? Will they lock those evil kids up for good?* The room was silent for a few minutes. Then, the noise of the doors swinging prompted him to sneak back up the stairs and peek out.

The big man had stepped closer to the stage and was standing there, clenching his fists. The old warrior moved to face him, putting his back to the double doors at the main entrance to the room, and he rested a hand on the pommel of his sword. The man in white joined the frontiersman, and they both faced the knight protector.

Is there going to be a fight? The acolyte was glad he wasn't in the middle of all of it. Especially since it seemed like his teeth were floating. *I need to hide until this feeling goes away. But what about the evil children?* He decided he could stay hidden for just a bit more.

The parson handed the writ he retrieved from his study to the old warrior. The knight protector shook his head, "Yes, I see that this is the same as the one I just reviewed. However, these are NOT the most current instructions."

"In the short time I've gotten to know you, I believe you to be an honest and sincere man," the parson retrieved his copy. "But without signed and written instructions to contradict these documents, they are binding."

"You don't understand—" the knight began.

"No, YOU don't understand." The big man stepped forward and poked his right index finger into the knight's chest. "These kids are my kin. Blood's thicker than water."

The frontiersman pulled a scroll from his belt with his left hand. "I know what I was told, and I got the paper to back it up. Yer not taking them anywhere." The big man loomed over the knight protector.

The knight forcefully slapped the big man's hand away from his chest. "The Darkness was upon them just two nights ago. Do you really think YOU can keep the Darkness from them?" the Knight challenged.

"Better than YOU!" the big man said as he shoved the Knight through the swinging double doors. The knight stumbled backward, and the big man followed. "There'll be no violence in my church!" The parson followed them through the double doors, which swung shut behind him.

The acolyte really wanted to know what happened, but the room was spinning now. *I hope those evil children get theirs. Need to lie down.*

He slowly crawled off the steps to the stage and carefully worked his way down the basement stairs. *Light hurts.* He blew out the lamp, stumbled to the darkest corner of the basement, and fell onto the bags of grain there.

I hope no one finds me. He closed his eyes, and darkness/blackness overtook him.

Still Small Voice

As the adults went into the church, Aiden, Ethan, and a handful of other children, their age ran after Sparkle Frog. There were occasional laughs and cheers from the adults at the tables as children almost caught the frog.

Meanwhile, Lauren's curiosity over what Uncle, Knight Protector, and Parson might be discussing overcame her shame at letting Sparkle Frog out. She tried to avoid catching anyone's attention as she made her way to the church.

Lauren looked back towards the field and saw Aiden stop dead and grab Ethan by his shirt. "Hey, E!" *Oh, no. Is this going to get worse?* She was torn between seeing what the men were talking about and keeping her brothers out of trouble.

"Stop holding me, Aiden!" Ethan cried as he twisted in Aiden's grip. "I want the candy!"

Lauren took a step in their direction, deciding she needed to intervene before there was more trouble.

"I do, too, but Sparkle Frog's too fast." Aiden seemed to ease up on Ethan. "I have a plan."

Aiden bent down and whispered his plan in Ethan's ear. Then the two boys ran off to the tall grass away from where the other children were chasing Sparkle Frog. *If Aiden has a plan, I'm sure it will work. I guess they can't get in too much trouble out in the tall grass.*

Lauren continued to the church, checking back over her shoulder to make sure they were staying out of trouble. The boys quickly found what they were looking for, raced back to the wagon, and hastily climbed into the back.

Lauren stopped to watch, and Ethan began yelling, "Sparkle Frog, I have a treat." Then he held something up in the air. The frog vaulted across the churchyard toward the treat. The other children yelled a collective, "Not fair!" Ethan pulled his arm back at the last second, and Sparkle Frog overshot Ethan's position on the wagon seat to land on a water barrel. *I can't believe that worked. That frog must really love Ethan.*

Ethan put his hand on the seat and waited for Sparkle Frog to come to him. Lauren assumed he must have a grasshopper or some other tasty treat for the frog because it leapt next to Ethan's hand. Ethan pulled his hand away, and Aiden brought the Frog's bucket down on top of it.

Aiden's plans always work. She marveled as Aiden scooted the bucket to the side of the seat where he had the lid waiting to push into position from below. He flipped the bucket over carefully to prevent jarring Sparkle Frog. Then held the bucket up for all to see.

The adults and children of the congregation let out a great cheer for the boys' victory. Lauren couldn't help but sigh in relief as that drama had finally ended on a positive note. *You know, we can handle things big and small.* The incident gave her confidence, so she straightened her shoulders and approached the doors, ready to state her case.

Suddenly the doors flew open, and Knight Protector stumbled out. Uncle followed, squaring off and facing the knight with his back to the wagon. Lauren found herself standing between the two of them.

"I told you if you laid hands on me again, there would be consequences." The knight drew his sword.

"I told you, these kids ain't going with you, no way, no how." Uncle grabbed Lauren roughly by the arm and pulled her behind him. "Lauren, you get behind me now. This here knight's done shown his true colors, claiming blood in a holy place!"

Lauren pulled away from Uncle and backed toward the wagon in disbelief. *Why would Knight Protector threaten violence on holy ground?*

"I don't buy into all this light/dark nonsense, but even I know better than to be threatening to draw blood on church grounds." Uncle moved to a wide fighting stance, looked over his should as if orienting himself for a moment, and slowly stepped backward toward the wagon. "This knight means to start a frackus, and I aim to oblige him! Aiden, bring me Ol' Faithful."

Lauren looked to the wagon, where Aiden stood frozen. *He must be just as confused as I am. What happened?*

Parson stepped between the two combatants. "Put that sword away. There will be no fighting on this holy ground!" A wave of relief flowed through Lauren.

Knight Protector obeyed and hung his head. Lauren saw the pink in his cheeks and felt that it must be from shame rather than being ready for a fight. "I was only trying to do what their father asked."

"The children's father bid they go to their grandmother's, and their uncle is here to fulfill that wish." Parson let out a deep sigh. Lauren saw the tension in his face dissolve. The men of the congregation stood, and those closest to Uncle closed ranks between the knight and the children. Their balled fists and stances told her they were ready for a fight.

"I apologize. I let the heat of the situation get the better of me." The knight held his hands palms up. "Clearly, their uncle is in the right without any documentation to prove otherwise." At this, the men of the congregation relaxed their hands but still kept between the kids and Knight Protector.

"You go right ahead and 'prove' otherwise." Uncle spat in derision. "But nobody other than their pa himself would convince me to let these kids spend another minute with you after you pulled a blade on me."

"Kids, we're leavin' for Grandma's house. Now!" Uncle called over his shoulder.

Lauren's mouth dropped. She didn't even get a chance to make her case. *They were really going to Grandma's house, even though the 'still small voice' told them to go to Blooming Glen.* How could she explain?

Uncle warily turned his back to Knight Protector and, as gently as his big hands could manage, ushered Lauren toward the wagon.

"Uncle, wait," she said.

"Daylight's a burnin', little one. We need to get on down the road." The hard look on his face made it clear he wasn't going to listen.

This made her angry, and she was about to push the issue. Then she realized that Uncle really didn't follow the Light, so anything she added right now would be met with skepticism. Grandma followed the Light, though. Grandma was very wise, and she listened to the children. *Maybe Grandma can help us avoid the consequences.*

"Boys, I'm going to use my 'still small voice' now." She hoped the boys would pick up on what she was trying to say. She climbed into the wagon and spoke to Aiden and Ethan quietly. "We need to go with Uncle to Grandma's house. Grandma can help us with Mama and Daddy. I know it."

"OK, Sissy, I hear your 'still small voice,'" Aiden replied just as quietly.

Ethan looked at Lauren with a raised eyebrow. "What did the voice say, Sissy?"

"I'll explain later. Just sit so we can go." They took their places in the wagon.

Lauren saw Knight Protector with his head hung and a frown on his face. He took a step forward. "The land North of Loggerton is believed to be in the grip of the Darkness."

Uncle turned back to the knight. "I just came that way; ain't no darker there than here." Lauren was reminded of just how dark it was here only a day ago. *Maybe we can help him see the Light on the way.*

"I implore you; the forces of Darkness are looking for these children. When you pass Loggerton, take the road to the east to Quinn's Ferry, then north to Burling Bridge, and on to Fairfields. The Light is strong on that route."

Uncle shook his head. "If you're any indication of what the Light has to offer us, then I'll pass." He turned back to the wagon and climbed the steps to the seat. "Before you get any ideas about coming along to help, forget it." Uncle pointed a thick index finger towards the knight protector. "I ain't sleepin' with one eye open worrying about you double-crossing me, yer high and mightiness." Uncle spat on the ground.

Lauren and the boys were settled on sacks of grain, with her in the middle of the two boys. Aiden's face was marked by a deep frown, and Ethan's lower lip quivered. She could tell they were both shaken up by all of this, so she placed her arms around them.

Uncle shook the reins, and the horses clomped off toward the road. The wagon turned, so the children were looking back toward the church.

Knight Protector called, "Remember to shine your light, children. If the Darkness proves too great on the north road, turn to Quinn's Ferry. You will find the help you need there."

With that, Knight Protector turned to Parson and appeared to be motioning to return to the church for a discussion. The men in the congregation stepped up protectively, but Parson waved them off.

The last Lauren saw of the church were the women getting up to clean the table with the men folding chairs while the children played tag. Her heart broke as she realized this might be the last time she'd see the little church on the hill. Her grief covered the pending dread about their journey into darkness. *If only Uncle could hear the 'still small voice.'*

18. Consequences

The sounds of physical exertion and feet scuffling across the stone floor of the church basement brought the acolyte to the edge of consciousness. He had a horrible headache, and his stomach was in agony.

He'd positioned himself in the darkest corner of the basement, hoping that was enough concealment to prevent anyone from detecting him. Even if it wasn't, he was in no shape to try to sneak around. He dared to open one eye to investigate and found even the little bit of indirect light from the open basement door to be excruciating.

That one glimpse revealed to him a group of men bringing tables and chairs down the steps and into the big open space in the basement. *Please don't find me. I can't get caught by these evil people.* He held his breath, hoping that might further conceal him in the darkness. If he could just stay still a little longer, he might remain undetected.

However, the knots in his stomach tightened, and he felt a sudden rush of saliva in his mouth. He caught a gag in the back of his throat and held back vomiting just barely.

He was wracked by another wave of nausea, and a cold sweat broke out over his whole body. He willed his body to cooperate and was able to hold out for what seemed an eternity.

He barely cracked his eyes, hoping the squint would prevent more pain in his head. Through the slits of his eyelids, he saw the last worker walk up the stairs and out the door, closing it.

The next wave of nausea and cold sweats hit, and he crawled to his knees onto the stone floor. Then he vomited violently. He held himself up and hoped the worst was passed. However, it was not, and he threw up again. His strength gave out, and he lay on his side, just barely avoiding the vile mess he'd just made.

The smell was horrible, and it made him want to wretch again. However, there was nothing left to vomit. The stone floor felt so nice and cool against his face. He wanted to just lie here forever. After a few moments, he faded back to oblivion.

***

He wasn't sure how long he had slept, but there was no longer any light coming from around the door to the basement. Opening his eyes didn't hurt anymore. He couldn't tell if that was from the lack of sunlight or if he was feeling better.

His intuition told him that the drink was bad by the smell of it. He really wished he had gone with that feeling. *It stinks so bad, and I'm so thirsty. I've got to get out of here before those evil people find me.* He carefully crawled onto his knees and then up the steps into the sanctuary. The room was barely lit by the light from a distant tower.

He was hungry again, so that was good. But he really needed water. There was still a loaf of bread. He decided to take it with him but to wait to eat until he found some water.

From his exploration earlier, he knew the only other place that might have water was the room on the other side of the main room he'd seen the parson go into.

He crawled up onto the stage and across to a door that went directly to the room. To the right, beyond the door, he found a tall crock sitting on a wooden stand with a spigot on it. Four tin cups hung from the stand. He took one and filled it, then drank greedily.

After gulping down the whole cup, a cold sweat crept over his whole body, and he lost the whole thing in another bout of vomiting. *Am I ever going to get over this sickness?*

He lay on his side for a few moments breathing slowly but deeply. His stomach calmed, and he gingerly sat up to get another cup of water. This time he sipped a small amount, swished it around in his mouth, and then spit it out. After repeating this two more times, he took a small sip and held it down.

How did I end up in this mess? Those evil children, that's how. As his mind turned over the events of the last couple of days, he stared blankly out the stained-glass window as he focused on the colorful pattern. Something in the corner of the room caught his eye.

He turned to look directly at the corner and saw a leather pack with a bright cloth rolled on top of it and a bedroll under the pack. *My pack! That's my pack!*

He crawled over to the pack, unclasped the cloth on the top, and unrolled it. It was a robe that appeared to be yellow; it was hard to tell in the colored light coming through the stained-glass window. With the sundown, the day had cooled off some, so he took a moment to put the robe on. It fits perfectly. *Yes, this is my pack. It has to have food in it.*

He got up on his knees and dumped the pack out. A rolled-up pair of pants hit the floor, and little pouches bounced out, too. He quickly tore two open and discovered beef jerky and nuts. *Should I eat, or will I just throw it up?* He ate one nut to see how it went.

While he tested his stomach, he looked through the rest of the contents of the bag. He found a small metal-bound box and a book. He took the box out and fumbled with the clasp. Inside, he found three glass globes with a dark cloudy substance inside and a cork on top.

He set the box on the floor, took one of the vials out of the box, and looked it over, not sure what to think of it. *I've had enough of strange liquids for today.* He set the vial on the floor next to the box.

His pack was now empty except for two cylindrical messenger cases—one attached to each side of the pack. He pulled one case out of the straps that held it in place and noticed the seal was broken.

Maybe this is a clue as to why I was fighting those evil children. Orders or something? The clasp was slightly bent, so as he pulled to open it, it stuck. He tried bending the clasp back into shape but didn't have the strength. Instead, he pulled on the strap as hard as he could. It broke free, and the released tension caused him to slam the case into the vial he had left on the floor.

The globe spewed out a puff of black smoke. *Oh no! What have I done?* The smoke curled up from the floor and expanded far larger and thicker than it should, considering the small size of the vial.

That's not right; I need to get out of here. He tried to stand up to get away from it but tripped on his robe and fell directly into the smoke. He inhaled a deep gasp of polluted air. His vision blurred, and as his consciousness began to fade, he thought, *Not again. How will I escape these evil people if I can't stay awake?*

19.On the road

The children huddled in silence in the back of the wagon as Uncle drove them northward. They made slow progress, being weighed down by all their provisions and the cow Clarabelle's plodding gait.

"Now listen here, it's gonna take us about a fortnight to get to yer gran's," Uncle called over his shoulder.

These were the first words he'd said since they'd left the church over an hour ago, so Lauren perked up to hear what he had to say.

"Now, I made this trip in four days, changing horses and running long and hard." He shook his head. "But you can't do that with all the provisions and such."

Uncle put the reins in one hand and turned to look at the children. "If there was some truth to all the Darkness talk, then we'll be overtaken quickly. If that happens, me and Ol' Faithful will handle it." He patted the head of his double-bitted axe.

"Yes, sir," Lauren found the boys saying with her in unison. *I don't think Uncle really knows what fighting the Darkness is all about.*

She looked at Aiden to see if he might be thinking the same thing and was surprised to see him making his way to sit next to Uncle.

"Do you think I could train Daddy Duck to land on my arm like a falcon?" Aiden asked.

"Now that's about the silliest thing I've heard in a while, youngster." Uncle chuckled as he tugged the reins left to avoid a rut. "I know that duck of yours is special and all, but you got two things workin' against you."

Aiden sat up straighter. "What are they, Uncle?"

"First off, a falconer gets them young, so they grow up being trained." Uncle looked down at Aiden fondly. "By his size, that duck's at least two years old. Have you ever heard the saying you can't teach an old dog a new trick?"

Aiden nodded. Lauren didn't like how Uncle was speaking down to Aiden about this. Daddy would have at least humored Aiden's request.

"Pretty sure that's true fer ducks too." Uncle redirected the horses back to the middle of the path. "Even if you did figure that out, the duck's got a real problem tryin' to act like a falcon."

"What's that, Uncle?" Aiden asked, looking up at the grizzled frontiersman.

"Webbed feet. They are all wrong for trying to land on yer arm. Even if you manage to get him to land on your arm, he doesn't have the talons a falcon has to grip it."

Aiden perked up. "That's why he always lands on my head!"

Lauren had to give Aiden credit for not letting Uncle's objections keep him down.

This made Uncle laugh a deep belly laugh. "Well, if you don't mind having a duck on your head, you can try to get him to come when you call."

"Thank you, Uncle!" Aiden gave Uncle a hug. "You're the best."

Lauren mulled this exchange over in her head, along with how things had ended with Knight Protector. Was Uncle just trying to get into their good graces, or was he being sincere? Could she really trust him?

***

The day ended as the western sky began to turn orange. Uncle found a flat patch of grass on the leeward side of a hill to park the wagon. He immediately put the children to work gathering kindling for the fire and water from a stream on the opposite side of the road.

Ethan wanted to complain about having to get water when they had barrels full in the wagon. However, he was a little bit afraid of Uncle after the way he shoved Knight Protector around. How would Uncle react to Ethan pushing back on his orders? So, he grudgingly took a bucket to the stream. When he got there, he saw many different water bugs and realized he should get some food for Sparkle Frog. He filled his bucket of water and returned it to the camp.

"Uncle, can I get some bugs for Sparkle Frog? "Ethan asked.

"Sure, try to find some nightcrawlers fer that duck, too," Uncle responded dismissively as he worked with Aiden to build a fire.

This acknowledgment pleased Ethan, and he decided Uncle might not be so bad after all. He scampered off to get food for the animals.

Ethan passed Lauren on her way back from the stream with water. As he chased after bugs, he noticed Lauren trying to milk Clarabelle. They didn't bring a milking stool, so she was forced to sit on her knees. Ethan laughed on the inside, watching her trying not to get her dress dirty. Girls were so silly.

As Ethan finished catching bugs, he noticed Uncle was doing something he had never seen before. He unrolled the tarp on the side of the wagon, leaving one side attached to the wagon. Inside the roll was a set of a dozen two-feet long black wooden stakes that were sharpened on one end, a length of black cord, and eleven little bells of black cast-iron.

"Uncle, what's all this?" Aiden asked as he inspected the items. Ethan came up beside them with bugs in his hands.

"There's lots of critters out here that could cause trouble, and you all think there's Darkness coming to get us." Uncle's grim look scared Ethan. "I can't go a fortnight

113

without sleep, so this is how we'll get warned if anything is comin' fer us."

"How does it work?" Aiden asked, inspecting the bells.

Uncle pulled a hammer out of the back of the wagon. "We make a circle out of these here stakes, then thread the cord around it." Uncle walked from the wagon out fifteen paces and hammered in a stake.

"Can I help?" Aiden held out his hands.

"In a minute. Just watch for now." Uncle picked up the stake and a mallet.

Ethan wanted to get a better view of what Uncle was going to do. He climbed awkwardly into the wagon, trying not to squish the bugs he had worked so hard to trap for Sparkle Frog.

Ethan watched Uncle pound stakes into the ground at even intervals in a circle around the wagon. He saved two stakes and put one at either corner of the tarp that was attached to the wagon to make a lean-to out of it.

Then Uncle picked up the cord and carried it to one of the stakes. He wrapped the middle of the cord around a notch in the stake two inches from the top. "Aiden, take this side of the rope and pull it tight to the next stake and wrap it just like this one. Then work around until we meet on the other side."

Aiden followed the instructions, and they met on the other side of the wagon.

"Now go hang a bell in the middle of the cord between the stakes," Uncle instructed.

Ethan had carefully dropped the bugs into Sparkle Frog's bucket. "I want to help."

Ethan jumped down from the wagon, and the boys followed Uncle's instructions and quickly had bells spaced around the perimeter. Ethan bumped the cord intentionally and found that it rang the bell on the section of the rope he hit.

When the boys were done, Uncle explained, "The whole thing is black, so it will go unnoticed in the dark." He bent to put his hand on the cord, "It's low enough to the ground that any kind of real danger will trip on it, but little critters like a field mouse won't set it off."

Lauren returned with her bucket of milk.

"Aiden, we need to get worms for Daddy Duck. Do you want to help?" Ethan called Aiden, who was stoking the fire.

"Yeah, E!" Aiden replied, hopping up to join Ethan. "Hey, Uncle, can we try to train Daddy Duck?"

"Go ahead," Uncle said dismissively as he placed a cooking rack over the fire. "Just put that cord on his leg and your wrist before you take the hood off."

Aiden went with Ethan to collect some worms and then climbed into the back of the wagon. Aiden saw Lauren hand Uncle a cast-iron pot with a wire hanger.

115

Uncle hung it over the fire. "Yer ma sure taught you right." Uncle complimented as he got out a wooden spoon to stir the pot.

Lauren smiled and gave a slight curtsy. "Thank you, Uncle."

Ethan's tummy rumbled.

The boys set the worms they caught on the wagon seat. Then, Aiden managed to get Daddy Duck out of the box without incident.

Ethan watched as Aiden tied the falconer's cord to Daddy Duck's leg and his own wrist. As soon as he removed the hood, Daddy Duck took to the sky and jerked Aiden's arm up with him. Aiden wobbled like he was going to fall off the wagon but then grabbed the wagon's side rail and steadied himself.

Ethan laughed at the wild display. After a couple of minutes of furiously trying to escape, Daddy Duck settled down and landed on the wagon seat. Then he let out an accusatory quack at Aiden, letting the boy know he was not happy with the current situation.

Before Aiden could respond, Daddy Duck noticed the worms on the seat. The frustrated duck let out another quack at Aiden and then picked up a worm in its bill and swallowed it. Then the duck nestled down on the seat and gobbled up another worm, keeping an eye on Aiden.

"Hate to say I told you so, but a duck ain't no falcon," Uncle called up gruffly from where he had taken a knee to stoke the fire.

"He's just getting used to the idea." Aiden gently patted the beleaguered duck on the back.

Daddy Duck repaid Aiden's kindness with an attempt to fly away again, giving Aiden a face full of feathers. Aiden lost his balance and fell, slamming his chin into the wagon seat.

He let out a cry of pain but recovered enough to sit-up on the floor of the wagon, brace his feet against the seat back and grab the cord attached to the duck with his other hand. Then he pulled the duck toward him.

Ethan broke out in laughter. Lauren stood frozen, and Uncle got up and stifled a laugh himself. He grabbed the duck in one of his big hands and pushed it down in place on the wagon seat.

Aiden let the cord go slack and picked up the falcon hood, and placed it on the duck. Then Uncle took the cord off its leg and put it back in the box.

"I know how much you like this duck," Uncle said as he helped Aiden from the wagon. "Next time you want to try that, get yer feet firmly planted on the ground."

"Yes, Uncle," Aiden responded with a frown.

"Let me look at that chin," Uncle said, turning Aiden's face. His chin was bright red with some bleeding superficial scrapes. Uncle got a handkerchief out of his pocket and dabbed at the scrapes.

"Told you, you can't train a duck to be a falcon. Now you got herself hurt, and you want me to kiss yer boo boo's like yer ma?"

Aiden's cheeks turned red, and he shook his head. He pulled away from Uncle.

Uncle knelt down to look Aiden in the eyes, "You need to man up and stand still. I need to clean this out so it don't get infected," Uncle said with obvious concern in his voice.

Lauren stepped between Uncle and Aiden. "May I?" She reached for the handkerchief.

Ethan's face flushed, and his blood boiled at how Uncle had treated Aiden. He was about to give Uncle a piece of his mind when he heard a thump in Sparkle Frog's bucket.

This reminded him how Uncle helped him with Sparkle Frog and that he wasn't usually mean to the kids. *Didn't Uncle warn Aiden that it wouldn't work?* Ethan paused, and his anger subsided. He decided this was just the *consequences* thing Daddy was always talking about, and Uncle just wasn't as nice as Daddy was about this kind of thing.

Lauren went over to one of the fresh buckets of water and soaked the handkerchief in it. Then she carefully dabbed at Aiden's chin. This wiped the blood clean. Then she rinsed it out in the bucket, folded it, and soaked it again.

She handed it to Aiden, "Now, just hold that on your chin for a few minutes. It will help with the swelling and keep you from bleeding all over the place.

Aiden nodded and followed her instructions.

The sun was nearly beyond the horizon, and the light from their roaring fire was stronger than the failing sunlight.

Uncle checked the pot to ensure it wasn't going to boil over. "It will be a while before we can eat."

"OK, Uncle," Ethan piped up, trying to get the group in a better mood. "What do we do now?"

"You and Lauren better get out the bedrolls and put them in the lean-to over there." Uncle pointed. "Prolly better change out of those Sunday school clothes too."

"Yes, sir!" Ethan responded and proceeded with Lauren to the back of the wagon.

Aiden sulked by the fire until his siblings were all done getting out the bedrolls and changing. Then he put the handkerchief in the water bucket and followed suit.

They ate a dinner of stew and hardtack. Then the children lay down in the lean-to, said their prayers, and snuggled up to go to sleep.

Ethan thought about all the events of the past week and could hardly believe all that had happened. He tried not to think about the Darkness that had nearly destroyed them.

He felt bad that they weren't going to save Mama, but maybe when they got to Grandma's house, she would listen. He was just glad Sparkle Frog got to come along. He needed his frog if they were going to have to keep fighting the Darkness. He just hoped that the Darkness wouldn't come for them tonight.

20. The Acolyte of the Dandelion Order

The youth awoke from the most vivid dream he could ever recall. The colors coming through the stained-glass window gave the room an otherworldly appearance. It took him a minute to gather his wits, but in full daylight, despite the colors from the window, he could now clearly see the whole room.

As he focused on his surroundings, he saw a black horn on the parson's desk. He knew that horn. It was the horn the bishop had in his dream. *The Horn of Power?* With a start, he realized he remembered. Not just the jumbled dreams of the past couple of nights but everything.

He looked down at himself and knew he was an Acolyte of the Dandelion Order. He was on an important mission with the bishop and that new kid: The Acolyte of the Violet Order.

That acolyte had betrayed them in favor of those evil children. The children—that girl and her brothers with the shield and flaming sword—attacked him and knocked him out. They would pay for that.

But where was the bishop? He could recall his flight through the woods and his troubles getting food in the church. But the bishop was nowhere to be seen. The bishop said he would deal with the parson. But the parson had been talking to the knight protector. So, what had happened to the bishop?

He clearly wasn't here. Some of his things were in the pile where the acolyte had found his pack. Had three kids killed the bishop?

Doubtful. But if they got that accursed light from the tower out of the protective sack the violet acolyte put it in before he turned sides, it could have caused some real issues for the bishop.

If he wasn't dead and he wasn't here, where would he go? Back to Loggerton? It was the closest full enclave of the new order. Even if the bishop had not gone to Loggerton, he might be able to find help there from other true believers. The acolyte needed to get there as quickly as possible so he could get help to deal with those evil kids.

He'd need some water and some more food before he did anything else. He went back to the water and carefully sipped a cup as he broke pieces of bread off the loaf he found on the floor and ate them slowly.

After he finished the second cup of water, he got up and looked at the pile of things around his pack. He saw the broken container and realized he had broken a Y'lohnu Sphere. This caused him a moment of panic.

The Y'lohnu Spheres were very special artifacts. He'd worked for two years to earn the dandelion robes and the right to learn to use the spheres. The bishop had just given them to him with the book on their use. Now he had broken one before he had even learned what they really do.

However, it occurred to him that it may have been breaking the Y'lohnu Sphere that caused his memory to return. It was said that the spheres could provide special knowledge to the true believer. *After a hit to the head, maybe my own knowledge is special.* That had to be it. It was unfortunate that this was his first use. However, regaining his true self had to be worth something.

He saw the case he was trying to open before he broke the globe lying on the floor. *Wait. Is this the document the knight protector had been arguing about?* He quickly popped the cap off the case and pulled out the document inside.

In the colored light of the room, he couldn't make out the words very well but noticed a clear sunbeam in the middle of the parson's desk. He got up and sat there, then unrolled the paper in the bright light.

A quick scan of the top of the document showed it to be a will. There were several sections outlining possessions, land, etc. The next section began:

Upon the death or disappearance of myself and my wife, one-year post-event, all these possessions are to be sold and put into a trust to be equally distributed to my daughter Lauren, son Aiden, and son Ethan until their majority. The trustee of this will and the children shall be their grandparents residing in Fairfields.

Those were the names of the evil children! This document was indeed the one the knight protector and the frontiersman were arguing over yesterday!

This section ended at the bottom of the page with a signature. It had a scribe mark he recognized from his own training. This page had been copied from another document in total. *But if this is a new document, it says what the frontiersman was saying. That doesn't make a lot of sense.*

He went back to his pack and pulled the second document out of its tube, and found it was a duplicate of the one he had just read. He sat back in the chair for a moment to try to understand what was going on. He noticed a rolled document on the parson's shelf with the same colored ribbons on the seal as the one he'd just read. He pulled it off the shelf and laid it out next to the other one.

These are the same, even with the same scribe mark. How can that be? There was a big argument over this document and different instructions. *I don't get it.*

He picked up the copy from his pack and realized there was more writing on the back. This surprised him as a scribe; he would never write on the back of a legal document. He laid it out and read:

Addendum: In the event of an unexplained death or disappearance, the children's guardianship shall be bestowed upon the Captain of the Mighty Mercenaries Blooming Glen cadre. The children are to be trained in the ways of the faithful service to the Light and the combat arts of the Mighty Mercenaries, until their majority, at the Blooming Glen garrison, where I am sure they will shine their lights over the whole wide world.

He sat with both hands on the desk, absorbing this new insight. *So, this is what the whole fight was about! The documents I was supposed to deliver had this addendum.*

It seemed odd that a parent would send their young kids to live in a garrison and be trained as soldiers. Then again, those kids were already powerful in whatever evil they were into. *Imagine if they were fully trained.* A cold wave of dread passed over his whole body.

I need to find the bishop; he'll know what to do. The tower here might still be shining, but there may still be a way to do something about it if he caught the evil kids. They had to go through Loggerton to get to Fairfields. The acolyte hoped he could find his mentor there.

They had a day's lead on him, so he needed to move quickly. He put the parson's document back on the shelf and stowed his belongings in the backpack, including the other copies of the writ and the Horn of Power. Now all he needed was a horse. He remembered tying off the horse at the children's farm before the battle.

That accursed tower! He wasn't sure what might await him if he went back there on his own.

As he contemplated this, he tied the ceremonial green cord around his waist and hoisted the backpack on his shoulders. He felt shaky for a moment. He wasn't sure he had overcome the previous day's ordeal yet.

He drank another cup of water and walked toward the front of the church. When he put his hand on the church's inner door, he heard the outer doors open.

Quickly, he went to the edge of the left sanctuary door and flattened himself behind it. The doors opened halfway, and the parson walked through, putting keys in a pouch on his belt as he walked toward his office.

When the spring-loaded doors swung shut, the acolyte snuck out into the foyer, hoping the parson wouldn't look behind him. Then the acolyte darted out the front door as fast as he could while making sure the front door didn't make any sounds to give him away.

Once outside, the sun's position told him it was between eight and nine in the morning. The parson had tied his piebald horse to a ring on a post outside the church. The acolyte untied the horse and leapt onto its back. Then he spurred it on toward the road to Loggerton. He hoped the speed of his theft would keep anyone from following.

He looked back a couple of times as he galloped away to see if the parson had come out to chase him. But he didn't see anything. Hopefully, his clean getaway would be the start of better luck. Maybe he would find the bishop and give those evil children what they deserved.

21. Brief Encounter

Lauren woke up from their restless night on the ground to the crackling of a fire. As she stirred, she realized that Uncle was already up tending to the fire. She gently woke the boys, and they all dressed in their work clothes, including a bonnet for Lauren. Something about that little touch to keep the sun off her face gave her a sense of normalcy despite their roadside camp. Uncle gave a few orders, and they were all off to chores with Lauren milking Clarabelle, j*ust like any other morning.*

When they finished their chores and breakfast, Ethan piped up, "We need to pray!" Lauren was shocked that they had forgotten to bless the meal. Father would never have let that happen. Things weren't as normal as she was starting to think.

Uncle took a sip from his coffee and waved his hand towards Ethan as if to say go ahead.

Lauren set her empty tin cup down and asked Ethan, "What are you thankful for?"

Ethan ran over and hugged Uncle. "I'm thankful for Uncle helping bring Sparkle Frog."

Uncle seemed to squirm under the hug, and his big eyes almost looked panicked by Ethan's sudden burst of emotion. He set down his cup and patted Ethan on the head. It surprised Lauren that Ethan was so affectionate after Uncle's treatment of Aiden the day before.

Aiden nodded his head. "I'm thankful Uncle helped bring Daddy Duck and that he teaches us stuff."

Lauren was not all that happy with Uncle's teaching methods. *He could have helped Aiden with the duck the day before to keep him safe.* She could feel heat in her cheeks, so she took a moment to compose herself. Then she picked up her kitten and petted him. "I'm thankful that Uncle let me bring Meow Meow."

Ethan let go of Uncle and stepped back, "What are you thankful for, Uncle?"

Uncle raised his eyebrows and sat there slack-jawed for a moment. "What? Why are you asking me?"

"Well, that's how we pray," Lauren said as she recognized they had put Uncle on the spot. "We find out what everyone is thankful for and thank God for it."

Uncle sat there blankly. "Well, I'm not sure about this God stuff. But I guess if there's something to be thankful for, it's that we got through the night safely. There's dangerous critters about. Cougars, bears, and such."

Ethan hugged Uncle again, "Oh, that's good! I'm thankful for that too." Ethan let go of Uncle and folded his hands. "Sissy, pray."

Lauren and the boys clasped their hands together and bowed their heads in reverence. Uncle absently stared into the fire while Lauren prayed. "Dear God, thank you for our pets and that they are with us on this journey. Thank you for Uncle teaching us things and keeping us safe. Please keep Mother and Father safe. Amen."

The boys said amen with Lauren; however, she didn't hear Uncle say amen. Father's deep bass "amen" always told them they were done. She learned to wait, head down, hands folded for that because sometimes he came up with more to say. It started to be an uncomfortably long time, and she was wondering what the boys were doing when she finally heard a grumbled "amen" come from Uncle.

"Come on. We're wasting daylight. We need to get a move on." Uncle poured a bucket of water on the fire and directed the children to pack up so they could get back on the road.

As the rock and creak of the wagon set in, Lauren had time to ponder their situation. She wasn't sure what to think about Uncle's lack of faith in the Light. It was clear he was uncomfortable with their customs, but he wasn't going to stop them from doing them. So that was good. *But when the consequences come...* Visions of fire and evil beasts sprang to life in her mind. *Will he finally be able to hear the 'still small voice'?*

***

The Dandelion Acolyte raced up North Road on his stolen horse. He was determined to reach Loggerton as quickly as possible. However, he was not a skilled horseman, so he quickly exhausted his horse, and it fell to a light trot despite his best efforts. After kicking the horse with his heels and snapping the reins fruitlessly, he accepted the horse's pace as the best he would get.

As the day wore on, he passed a place that appeared to have been a campsite the night before. The grass was matted down, and there was a damp fire pit. It was near a stream that seemed appropriate for watering his horse, so he stopped to investigate. While the horse was drinking, he filled a waterskin that was tied to the saddle and drank. He looked around intently for clues as to who might have stopped here. There were holes in the ground in a large circle around the fire. There were clearly places where the grass was flattened, and many different footprints dented the dirt.

He wasn't a professional tracker, so he couldn't tell for sure exactly how many people there were. It was clear it was a group with a wagon based on the indents in the grass from the wheels. He noticed three different sizes of footprints that only children could make. *It's them!*

Dread welled up from the pit of his stomach. It was so strong he hoped he wouldn't throw up. If they could destroy a Y'lohnu Censer and hellhounds, what could they do to me if I ran into them on my own?

He stood for a moment, questioning whether to continue to Loggerton. If the bishop was there, he might have formulated a plan for running into the children again. If he wasn't, the acolyte could still hide with the enclave there—strength in numbers. He just had to get past them without really drawing their attention.

I wish I'd studied geography more diligently. The only route he was aware of was just to stay on North Road. Shaking his head in acceptance of certain doom, he mounted his horse and continued.

As the day wore on, he was able to figure out a good rhythm with the horse. He got it to travel at a good pace for an extended period if he alternated a slow trot with a fast one. By midafternoon, he could see a wagon pulled by two horses with a cow trailing behind it. This was it. It had to be the children and a big man. He pulled up short because he didn't believe they had seen him, and they were cresting a rise.

He waited, considering his next move. He had to get past them without alerting them to who he was. Looking around him, neither side of the road was good for his horse to travel on. There were too many brambles and bushes. He had to take the road. He could hold back and wait for night or race past them and hope they did not recognize him.

Every minute of delay was less time for him to find the bishop and warn him of their approach. *I must go now!*

* * *

By midafternoon, Lauren heard hoofbeats behind the wagon. She looked to see a horse running at top speed, carrying a rider in a yellow robe. Lauren patted her uncle on the shoulder. "Look!"

Uncle turned his head at her insistence.

The rider was moving fast. Lauren couldn't tell if that meant ill or good for them. She saw Uncle reach to his side and pick up Ol' Faithful and lay it across his lap. *Is this dangerous? Would a minion of the Darkness be riding in full daylight?* Lauren realized her spear was out of reach, and she couldn't grab it without alerting the rider to her intentions.

Something about those yellow robes seemed familiar, but the rider was going so fast she couldn't really tell. Lauren took a deep breath to drive out the tension enveloping her body. *God, is this an enemy I need to attack?* She waited, but the feeling of power she got when she used her spear didn't come. She took another deep breath, and the rider was past them before she let it all the way out.

Uncle put Ol' Faithful back. "I wonder what that was all about? What's going on out here that somebody needs to be in such an all-fire hurry?"

Aiden patted Lauren's shoulder. "Sissy, did that person seem familiar to you?"

"I'm not sure, Aiden," Lauren replied. "It's possible, but I couldn't really tell."

She squinted up the road after the rider. "I thought that the robes looked like the Dandelion Acolyte's, but he was moving so fast I couldn't tell if there were tassels on the bottom or not."

Aiden looked up and away towards the Tower of Light, "I couldn't tell either, but didn't he leave his robe in the mud by our house?"

"Well yeah, I guess that's right, so it couldn't be him," Lauren nodded, dismissing the idea that it was the acolyte they'd fought.

"What's this about an acolyte?" Uncle asked.

Ethan clamored through the wagon and hopped on the driver's seat beside Uncle. "The other night, the bishop and the yellow acolyte and the bad dogs came to our house and attacked us. Sissy knocked out the acolyte with her spear."

"Knocked out the acolyte with your spear, you say?" Uncle cocked his head and raised an eyebrow.

"She conked him on the wonkus." Ethan slapped his palm on his forehead. "And he fell down, but then when we came back, he was gone."

"She hit him with the spear, and then he was gone." Uncle's tone betrayed his skepticism. "Is that what you're trying to tell me?"

"That's what happened, all right!" Ethan nodded vigorously, with his big puppy dog eyes shining.

Lauren could tell her brother wanted Uncle to accept his story as the truth. Deep down, she wanted that too.

Uncle shook his head and turned back to the reins.

Aiden whispered in Lauren's ear, "I don't think he believes us."

Lauren nodded. "I don't think he does either."

Uncle called over his shoulder, "Why don't you children just keep your fairy stories fer yer gran? I'm sure she'll be more than happy to tell you a yarn of her own, all right."

Ethan turned to Lauren, and she shook her head. "Yes, sir," she said.

Ethan's lower lip folded down in a pitiful pout, and he clamored back to his seat in the back of the wagon.

But she wasn't sure what to think about the rider with yellow robes. *Maybe it was the acolyte? But would he even be up and about yet?* After they hit their friend Nicolas with the spear, it took Sparkle Frog and Meow Meow's special gifts to wake him. Even then, he didn't remember who he was. That just couldn't be the Dandelion Acolyte. But if it was, what danger could be lurking ahead for them?

* * *

After putting a small hill between him and the wagon, the acolyte slowed the horse to a canter. *It was them! It was the evil children, and I made it past them without incident!*

They were clearly headed to Loggerton. It was the only destination on this road. With the enclave there, he could set a trap for them.

Based on how quickly the horse outpaced them, the acolyte was sure he could stay ahead of them. It would give him time to warn the bishop. Then they could mount a proper defense before the evil children would arrive. What he really needed was a way to slow them down or even stop them from moving forward so that he could raise forces to come attack when they weren't expecting it.

Wait, I have the book of the Dandelion Order and Y'lohnu Spheres. I'm sure I can find a way to thwart the evil children and the big man too.

The acolyte rode as long after dark as he dared. When he felt his horse could go no farther, he crossed a bridge and walked his horse to the edge of a stream. He built a fire with a combination of moonlight and the distant Tower of Light.

He hated the golden light of the tower, but he had to admit that it proved useful in getting his camp together. *It should be the red light of the Y'lohnu Censers, the true light.* In the heat of his seething hatred, he ate a light dinner and fed the horse.

He skimmed through the Book of the Dandelion Order, looking for secrets that might help him attack his foes. He found a chapter on animals and how to influence them. The chapter described using the contents of a Y'lohnu Sphere to enhance the water that they drank. An animal in this condition would be susceptible to human influence and instruction in a supernatural way.

What would happen if I enriched the water their horses were drinking? He opened the box of Y'lohnu Spheres and examined one carefully before putting it back in the case. He doubted he could get close enough to their horses without being seen. He could try to get upstream and affect them that way, but that would require a censer.

He picked the book back up, but eventually, sleep took him before he found an answer. Deep into the night, he was awoken by screams from his horse. He jerked up and onto one knee next to his pack and the open box of Y'lohnu Spheres.

The fire had died down to a pale glow, but on the far side of the embers, he could see a cougar crouched and looking for an opening to attack his rearing horse. *No! I need to get to Loggerton. I can't lose my horse!*

Reflexively, the acolyte reached about for something, a stick, a rock, anything to distract the cougar away from the horse. All his groping hands found was a Y'lohnu Sphere. The cougar leapt towards his horse. Lacking anything better to use as a weapon, he threw the globe with all his might, and it hit the animal's nose.

The globe's thin glass shell erupted upon contact with the cougar. Black smoke enveloped the large cat, and it went limp in midair. The horse side-stepped out of the way as the beast's dead weight slammed into the ground.

"I got it! I got it!" The acolyte's cry rang out across the countryside. *Did I give myself away?* His head jerked left and right, and he peered south. *That's silly. I'm well beyond them. They couldn't possibly hear.*

He stoked up the fire and then went to investigate the cougar. It was unconscious, breathing heavily. *Good, it's not dead.* From what he'd read earlier, this sleeping state could persist for just a few minutes or a few hours, based on the creature.

He checked on the horse, and thankfully it hadn't been hurt. "Good girl, easy now." He patted the horse, but it remained very skittish, and he realized he needed to move the cougar, or the horse would never calm down.

With a great amount of exertion, he dragged the beast to the far side of the fire from the horse. Then he sat down and found the chapter on controlling animals, which indicated that he only needed to visualize exactly what the animal should do and then speak his intent.

How would a cougar understand my words? The book said the enlightenment of the smoke was transcendent, that it would give you power beyond imagination. One only had to be in tune with the Y'lohnu light, and the globe's smoke would do the rest. The text indicated that the closer to the creature's natural intent, the more surely it would comply.

The acolyte knelt beside the cougar and tentatively put a hand on its head. He visualized the cougar assaulting the frontiersman. "Hunt the big man. Eat his cow and horses." He tried to visualize the cougar devouring the animals.

The bishop would want to deal with the children himself. It took him a moment to picture the cougar menacing the children without attacking them. "Hold the children until I arrive, don't attack them."

He repeated this multiple times to the slumbering beast and intently watched for it to react in some way. *I hope this works. They will never suspect this coming.* He leaned against a tree to continue his vigil, but despite his best efforts to stay alert, he dozed off.

As dawn came, the sunlight woke the acolyte. The cougar stirred as well. It rose with a glassy, vacant look and didn't acknowledge the acolyte or his horse's presence. His horse whinnied and stamped in the direction of the cougar. But it merely crouched and began stalking slowly towards a small rise overlooking the stream. This caused his horse to settle down.

It worked! The acolyte watched the cougar top the rise and followed discretely behind it. He found it settled in on its haunches, slowly scanning its head left and right. The acolyte worried for a moment that his instructions were not understood by the beast, but then he realized the rise was the perfect place to watch for prey.

He wasn't sure how effective the beast would be at stopping its prey. They were a day behind now and likely two by the time he got to Loggerton. But if the beast could slow them down, even better. It might prevail where the bishop had not. With that hope in his mind, he packed his meager possessions and rode his horse with haste to Loggerton.

22. Predator

As dusk settled in, the wagon passed a hillock overlooking the road. Uncle thought he saw movement in the tall grass out of the corner of his eye, but it was gone when he looked in that direction. He rubbed his eyes and peered more intently but found nothing. Shaking his head dismissively, he began to look for a creek running near the road with a nearby open space to park the wagon and set up camp.

He found a nice spot with a still-damp fire pit. It must have been from the rider the day before. He seemed to have spooked the kids. Better not say nuthin.

The kids hopped to their chores like clockwork, and the camp seemed to set itself up. Aiden tried to train his duck without any more success than before. *Obstinate boy. You can't train no duck to be a falcon.*

Uncle really wanted to tell the boy to give up on the fool's errand. But as he began to open his mouth, he remembered that time he thought he could fly hanging from a kite out of the barn. *How many times did I try that?*

Aiden carefully put the duck on the ground and then went through the motions of trying to get the bird to fly on command. *That Aiden's not one to give up on something lightly. Guess the boy's kin, after all.*

Uncle turned to his task at hand of building a fire. He noticed some tiny shards of glass and what looked like big cat tracks near the fire pit. No blood or carcasses, so there wasn't a fight. *Critter must have been scared away by the fire. Better make it BIG tonight if there's a puma about.*

As the evening turned to night, he made sure the children were in bed, then stoked the fire as large as he dared. He settled himself with his back to a tree inside the ring of bells. A cloud crossed the moon, putting the camp into its darkest state of the night. *Definitely needed that big fire.* He laid his double-bitted axe across his lap and slowly nodded off to sleep.

***

Lauren woke to Meow Meow licking her nose. She swatted at the little kitten before she realized it was her pet. When she opened her eyes, she could vaguely make out Meow Meow's white spots.

"How did you get down here?" Lauren whispered. How had he gotten out of the back of the wagon? She'd put him in a box.

Suddenly Lauren heard a jingling bell outside the lean-to. *Danger!* Adrenaline rushed through her, followed by a warm wave that prickled her skin. Aiden and Ethan both awoke with a start. Lauren poked her head out of the lean-to to see what caused the alarm.

Outside, Uncle jumped to his feet with more speed than might be expected of such a large man. He held his axe ready, his head scanning back and forth.

The campsite was in near-total darkness except for the circle around the dying fire. The bell rang again, and Lauren pinpointed where it was. Uncle moved between her and the direction of the bell.

The fire was to Lauren's left, so she covered that eye. In the distance, she caught sight of the dying fire in the eyes of a predator slinking toward the campsite.

"Uncle, do you see it?" Lauren hissed as quietly as she could.

"Kids, you get up in that wagon and stay out of sight." He held the ax right near the head. "We've got a dangerous predator out here,"

Lauren turned toward the wagon to obey and saw the boys doing likewise, almost like it was day. *Our weapons are glowing. That creature isn't just some predator. It's of the Darkness!*

She clambered up into the wagon and grabbed her spear. "Uncle, the creature has Darkness in it. I can help with my spear."

"This ain't no time for yer fairy stories," he yelled as the cat came more clearly into view. Uncle began to match its movements.

"What do we do, Sissy?" Aiden whispered.

She felt a moment of doubt about disobeying Uncle's orders, but God wouldn't give her the power if it wasn't important. "Be ready to help if you can." Lauren lifted her glowing spear, ready to throw. *God help my aim to be true.* Lauren watched the cat back off slightly, and she wondered if it might be rethinking its choice of meals.

Without warning, it pounced. Uncle stood his ground with his axe in a wide two-handed grip. As the beast closed the gap to bite his neck, Uncle jammed the wooden handle of his axe into the cougar's open mouth.

Uncle held the axe at shoulder length, which was high enough that the cougar could barely keep its back feet on the ground. It flailed its forelegs, swiping at Uncle to free itself.

"No! Not Uncle! Sissy, do something!" Ethan pulled on Lauren's nightdress.

Uncle swayed to the right, which turned the beast's body into Lauren's view. At that very moment, she felt the power well up in her, and she released her spear. *God, please help it strike true.* The blue-light spear tip buried itself into the cougar's head just as Uncle forced his right arm up high, and the shaft of the spear dropped to the ground.

Uncle's movement to the left obscured the creature's fall. He quickly followed with an axe strike to the ground in front of him that she couldn't see. Uncle turned to them and stepped to the side. "This cat's a goner. Good thing you all stayed up there. This was dangerous business."

Lauren let out a deep breath she didn't even realize she was holding. *Thank you, Lord!*

"Sissy, you did it! You saved Coo Coo." Ethan gave her a big hug.

"What do you mean she saved me? It was Ol' Faithful here that done the savin'."

Lauren quickly realized that the boys were still armed but lacked any of their holy light. But hadn't Uncle seen her spear hit the cougar?

"Didn't you see, Coo Coo?" Ethan began.

"The only thing I see is a couple of little boys playin' soldier and a girl who ought to know better 'n' to be rilin' them boys up." Uncle strode toward the children. "I told you three to get up in the wagon and hide. I didn't say anything about arming for battle."

Uncle pointed an accusing finger at them. Something about the red glow from the fading fire made it feel worse than it was. "You were drawing attention to yourselves up there waving swords around. Put that stuff down before you hurt yourself."

This was going very badly. *How had Uncle not seen the spear?* "Please don't be angry with them, Uncle. I was worried that the cat might get past you. I told them to get out the weapons."

Uncle stepped up to them and put the head of the double-bitted axe on the ground while he leaned on the handle. "Ain't no critter here in these parts that Ol' Faithful can't get the better of. Next time I tell you to go hide, I mean go hide. I can't fight well if I have to worry about you coming up to try to help. Got it?"

"Yes, sir," Lauren replied sheepishly, and the boys just nodded.

Uncle pointed at them, "Now put those things away and get back to bed."

"Yes sir," they all responded despondently.

The boys put their arms away and followed Lauren down from the wagon while Uncle walked to the fire. He added small branches to it and stoked it up considerably. Uncle dragged the cougar's carcass closer to the flames and began to skin it.

In the lean-to, Aiden whispered, "Sissy, why didn't you tell Uncle about the spear? It looked like you knocked the cougar out before he flipped it over and killed it."

"Yeah, Sissy? Why let Coo Coo take all the credit?" Ethan whispered.

How could she explain this to the boys? *God, you gave us these gifts. Why don't people believe?*

"He doesn't believe in the Light," Lauren started in a low whisper, "I think he would have been very cross if he realized that I actually threw my spear in his direction."

"I didn't think about that," Ethan nodded.

"But, Sissy, that's not honest." Aiden pointed in the direction of the Tower of Light. "Won't that hurt the light from the tower?"

"Ethan was honest. Uncle just didn't believe." Lauren frowned as she thought about this. *We told him the truth about real power, something that happened right in front of him, and he didn't believe it.* "I think it's up to us to be honest, but if he doesn't believe, that's not our fault."

Aiden shook his head in agreement. "Yeah, I guess that's right."

Lauren lay down on the bedroll. "He's a proud man. He thinks he did it on his own, so I guess it's better for now not to challenge it."

"Maybe Grandma can help us tell him the truth." Ethan offered as he took his own place.

"Yeah, Grandma will know what to say." Aiden joined them in the bedroll.

Lauren closed her eyes and sighed. *Uncle is so stubborn. But maybe Aiden's right. Maybe Grandma will know what to say.*

Soon the boys' breathing slowed to indicate they were fast asleep. It was hard for Lauren to sleep. While she appreciated that Uncle was protective of them, she wondered if his disbelief would be an issue in the future. He may very well have been able to defeat the cougar on his own, despite it being a creature of Darkness. *Could Uncle really defeat something more dangerous—a hellhound or a group of the bishop's people?* She hoped the cougar was their consequence for not following the 'still small voice' to Blooming Glen. If not, they had to find a way to help Uncle see the Light before a worse confrontation occurred.

23. Bath Time

After corrupting the cougar, the acolyte made haste for Loggerton. Driven by the desire to marshal forces against the evil children and a need for basic food and shelter, he pushed the horse to its limits. After two and a half days of hard riding, Loggerton came into view.

He immediately pulled his mount up short. *Something's not right.* He scratched his head as he surveyed the town. This didn't relieve the itch, but it was forgotten when he saw the colorful welcome tent was no longer pitched in front of Loggerton's lone church, and the censers the bishop had placed outside the chapel were gone as well. While it felt off, it also looked brighter and cleaner than he remembered.

The red light of the Y'lohnu Censers is GONE! Did the evil children beat me here? Impossible. Something else was going on. He had to find out what. As he prepared to kick the horse's flanks to continue his investigation, his doubts overtook him. *All trace of the bishop's work here is missing; I need to be careful.*

If there was some kind of coup, then his position as an acolyte might make him suspect. As an orphan, the only people who might recognize him were at the orphanage. It might be better if he hid his allegiance while he learned what was really going on.

There was also the off chance that a messenger pigeon had come this way with word of him stealing the parson's

147

horse. The piebald's pattern was very distinctive. If he rode into town, he realized he might run afoul of the sheriff. So, he turned his horse off the road and into the woods a half-mile from Loggerton. He found a spot of grass near a creek and tied the horse up with as much lead as he could give it. Despite his hard ride, he had grown fond of the horse. "Don't worry. I'll be back as soon as I know what's happened to the bishop's work here."

He looked down at his robe and ceremonial belt. *This will never do for sneaking around. Better to look like a beggar.* He carefully removed and packed his robe, belt, and sandals. His pants were still filthy, but as he looked himself over, he found that the rest of him was fairly clean. Although a quick sniff told him, his hard traveling made him smell like a beggar. He felt his head and knew that his hair was out of control as well, and his scalp itched.

As he headed for town, he found a patch of dirt and picked up a couple of handfuls. He rubbed it into his hair, face, and body. More itching on his scalp. Maybe he had plenty of dirt in his hair as it was. He hoped this made him quite a pitiful sight and would be enough of a disguise while he scouted the town.

He approached from the woods and came upon the back of a stable. There was a board missing at the bottom of the wall. He inspected it and decided he'd need to break out a board to fit. *Too bad, it would have been good to have a place to hide.*

As he rounded the corner of the stable onto the main street, he saw the town was bustling with industry. While

Loggerton wasn't much more than a village, farmers from all over brought their goods to trade. The sawmill on the river that gave the town its name was in full use.

On his way to investigate the chapel, he passed the inn attached to the stable and heard a loud "Oh, my goodness!"

He turned to see a matronly woman in her forties in a simple gray linen smock dress and a white apron standing on the inn's porch, limply holding onto a rug she had been shaking out. They made eye contact, and suddenly the acolyte went cold from head to foot. *No! I've been found out already!*

"Young man!" she cried out. "You look like you've been dragged through the gates of hell. You come here this instant, and let me help you!"

The woman dropped the rug and began walking toward him. He froze, not sure whether to fight or flee. The look of deep concern on the woman's face told him that she was no threat. *Is this some kind of trick? Why would a stranger want to help me?*

When she reached him, she put an arm around his shoulder and turned him towards the inn. The gentle warmth of her arm on his shoulder overcame his skepticism. *What harm could this old woman do? Maybe she'll feed me.* With his free arm, he scratched his itchy scalp. *A bath would be good, too, if I can find a new disguise.*

They walked into the inn. The wooden floor was well-worn, and roughhewn wooden benches and tables filled the room. Sunlight streamed through the windows and door, illuminating the space and the low ceiling in the common room. There was a large cast-iron stew pot hung over a cheery fire in the large fireplace on the wall. To his right, he saw a bar that was curiously absent of any casks or bottles. To the left and the right of the fireplace were wooden doors to other rooms, and the back of the common room had two curtained alcoves separated by stairs leading up.

"Look here, young man. You need a good washing worse than my pigs do." The matron sat him down on a bench facing a long table in front of the fireplace. "But it also looks like you haven't had a good meal in your whole life." She shook her head with a frown. "I'm going to see you get some food and then a good bath."

He itched his head again. *A bath would be good to get rid of this infernal itching. But this dirt's my whole disguise!* She went to the fire and dipped a large spoon in the pot and took out some stew, and sipped at the edge of the ladle. She shook her head, reached into a spice bowl on the mantle, sprinkled some into the stew, and stirred. She took down a bowl, filled it, and brought it to him with a wooden soup spoon. "That's hot now. You just wait until I get back with some bread and milk."

He gave her a slight nod and scratched his head. *Better to say nothing than give something away.* She went off behind the bar and through a doorway into the kitchen.

While she was gone, he contemplated making a run for it. But the aroma of the warm stew kept him bolted in place. His hunger overcame the matron's warning, and he tried a spoon full, burning his tongue. *Ouch! Dummy, she said it was hot.*

That didn't completely deter him. He took another spoonful and, this time, blew on it a few times and sipped the broth off slowly before taking a bite of meat. It was the best food he'd had in days. But it would have been better without the burned tongue.

He saw the matron returning with a big tray of food hiding her face. He hastily dropped the spoon and folded his hands on the table.

She set down the tray containing three dinner rolls, a pitcher of milk, a mug, and a brown kiln-fired clay bowl of butter with an iron-bladed butter knife stuck into it.

He reached for a roll, and she swatted his hand. "Young man! I know you must have been through some trials, but now's not the time to be forgetting the Lord who put me in your path today to provide this meal."

This stopped him cold. Was she really going to hold him up to say grace? Her raised eyebrow, and pursed lips told him that was true. However, he wasn't sure how he should pray, given the changes to the church outside.

Coming off as mute would keep people from asking too many questions. He merely clasped his hands together, bowed his head, and waited. Would she take the hint?

The waiting was excruciating because he really needed to itch his head. He could smell the warm rolls, and he knew the butter was freshly churned. How long would it take for her to figure it out? After what felt like an eternity, he slowly raised his head and opened an eye.

"It's all right, son," she walked around the table and patted his head. He looked up at her, and she consoled, "The Lord knows your heart."

The acolyte snatched a roll, tore it in half, spread a generous dollop of butter on it, and shoved it greedily into his mouth.

"You're a hungry one now, aren't you?" She stood and watched as he gobbled up everything on the tray and the bowl of stew in just a couple of minutes. "Normally, I would chastise a young man for eating so fast, but you must have been near starved to death. Do you need more stew?"

He nodded vigorously. *She bought the mute act. That should save me some trouble explaining myself.* Tension he didn't realize was there oozed out of his neck and back. He let out a deep sigh. Then he scratched his itching head. *A bath sounds so good, but I can't lose this dirty beggar look if I want to scout the town. I need to get rid of her so I can sneak out before she makes me take a bath.*

She seemed to be waiting for something. *Maybe to clean up after me?* He drank the last of the broth from his bowl, placed it on the tray, looked up, and smiled. He patted his stomach.

"I'm glad you liked it." She cleared the table onto the tray and took it back to the kitchen. As soon as she was out of sight, he got up and snuck towards the door.

The church bell began ringing for noon. He stopped in place to check if she was coming out. When he realized she was still in the kitchen, he turned to bolt out the door.

A dozen rugged muscular men in blue denim overalls and long-sleeved, cotton button-down shirts began to file into the inn. As he looked for an opening to duck out the door between them, he heard, "Young Man! You are in no condition to be going out in public. You come right here; you're getting a bath!"

Too late! The acolyte froze, hoping the dirt on his face muted the red in his cheeks. The men coming into the room chuckled.

A shorter man in the middle of the group spoke up. "Go on, boy. Get yourself a bath before she makes me take one for getting dirty just lookin' at ya."

The rest of the men laughed louder, and the acolyte's face grew hotter.

"Come on now, don't listen to them." The matron grabbed him by the elbow and turned him toward the door on the left side of the fireplace. He scanned the room, looking for another way out. The itching hit again, and he scratched feverously.

"Land sakes, boy!" The matron turned him so his back was to her and then started picking through his hair. "Oh no, you've got lice!"

The men in the room roared in laughter. The acolyte's face went red. *They'll get theirs when the bishop comes back.* The matron grabbed his elbow and pulled him towards the door. "Come into the washroom quick. I've got a tonic for the itch."

When they entered the small room, he surveyed it for another way out. All he found was a large tin box with a pipe going into the top, which was attached to the back of the fireplace from the great room. A spigot protruded from it and hung above a metal bathtub. The far wall had a bar with lightweight, hooded white robes hanging from it, and below them were two feet by two feet cubbies filled with towels and sandals. Next to the tub sat some rough brushes and a clay bowl with a couple of bars of harsh lye soap. *No way out but the way I came in. But she's right; I need to get the lice taken care of.*

She sat him down on a three-legged stool next to the tub and bent his head back over it. "I'm sorry, son, but the hair's got to go." He looked up to see her over him with a wicked-looking set of scissors.

His eyes bugged out at the sight of the iron shears. *She's not chopping off my hair!* Another wave of itchiness hit him, and it took all he had not to reach up and scratch the skin off his head. *I guess if that's what she's got to do, that's what she's got to do.*

He nodded almost imperceptibly, and she began to hack away at his hair. In short order, she had him trimmed to just a stubble. Then she got out a straight razor and finished the job. By the time she was done, where his head didn't itch, it stung.

"Hold on now. I'm going to get the tonic." She left his field of view, and he proceeded to scratch at the hairless top of his head. She came back with a container with blue liquid in it and poured some in one hand, set down the container, and rubbed her hands together. Then started massaging the tonic into his head.

The relief was instant. He let out a deep sigh and was worried she might now question his mute act. But she said nothing, and he let her continue. When she was done, she patted the back of his head. He took the hint and stood up.

"I'm so sorry to add to your rough treatment in the world." She shook her head as she looked him over. "Maybe this is the fresh start the good Lord had for you, hair and all."

He thought about that for a moment and realized that it might not be so bad after all. From a distance, nobody would recognize him.

The Matron turned the spigot, and hot water flowed into the bathtub. There was another pipe coming down from the ceiling with a valve on the bottom, pointing into the tub. She turned it, and it seemed like that must be cold water. "This will take a few minutes to fill up. I'm making it a little hotter than you might like, but you need a good soak."

He could tell by the steam coming off it that the bath was definitely going to be hotter than he liked.

She continued, "Go over behind that screen and take off your pants and throw them over so I can burn them." She pointed to a screen set in the corner. "When you're done,

155

you can change into a robe, pants, and sandals. You can keep them till we can find you a proper outfit."

She pointed to the cubbies in the wall,

The robes! That's it! I'll keep the hood up and my head bowed. They aren't a proper color, so no one will suspect I'm with the bishop.

A deep sigh left him unexpectedly. This was going to work. His head felt better, and a hot bath would be just the thing to work out the aches and pains of the hard ride. He followed her instructions and waited behind the screen until she left the room. Then he slowly eased himself into the too-hot water and felt the aches and pains melt away.

He soaked until the water began to run cold, then rushed to clean himself. He dressed in the clothes provided and pulled the hood over his head. He peeked out into the dining hall. The accursed workmen were gone, and the matron was nowhere to be seen. *Now's my chance!*

He dashed for the front door and ran directly into the matron, who was carrying a basket of vegetables. "Well, now, where do you think you're getting off too?"

Trapped. He'd done a good job of avoiding her questions so far, and he preferred to keep it that way. Just then, the church bell rang a single chime for one o'clock in the afternoon. On a hunch, he pointed out the door towards the church. He put his hands together and bowed his head like he was praying, then repeated the actions for emphasis.

"Well, now, aren't you a devoted one?" she said. "Parson's out and about visiting old folks today, reassuring them the Light's as strong as ever after all the chaos here the past few weeks." She put her hands on her hips, clearly blocking his passage. "Likely won't be back until Wednesday's services."

The acolyte's eyes bulged, and his mouth dropped. The bishop locked up the parson for heresy! Now he was back in charge? He realized his reaction might give him away, so he quickly bowed his head and reached to take the basket from her.

"You seem like a good boy, all full of the Light despite your troubles." She handed him the basket. "I could use a little help around here, peeling potatoes, washing dishes, and such. How about you help me out for a few days, and I'll keep you fed and give you a bed. Then when the parson returns, we can see about ways he can help. Would you like that?"

Lacking any other real options, the acolyte nodded. The inn was busy for lunch and likely more so for supper. *If I bide my time, I'll catch all the town gossip and find out what the parson did to get free. Then he'll get his along with those evil kids if the cougar didn't get them first.*

He followed her to the kitchen as a smile of grim satisfaction split his face ear to ear.

The morning after the cougar incident, Ethan woke to find the cougar hide stretched on a wooden frame Uncle must have made in the night. He was in the process of pouring salt on the skin when Ethan pulled on his shirt. "Whatcha doin', Coo Coo?"

Uncle paused his task, "I'm curing the cougar hide. I'm gonna sew it into my cloak."

"Oh, that will be scary, Coo Coo." Ethan took a step back from Uncle's grisly prize.

"That's the idea." Uncle squatted down to make sure he had salt evenly covering his prize. "Nobody's gonna mess with somebody done killed a cougar with their bare hands."

"Sissy helped." Ethan shoved his fists on his hips and pursed his lips in indignation.

"Yah, yah, the Light and all that." Uncle waved a hand dismissively as he stood back up and put the bag of salt in the back of the wagon. "I got faith, little one." He picked up his axe and showed Ethan the cougar's teeth marks embedded in the handle. "This here's Ol' Faithful. I got faith that there ain't no man nor beast gonna do harm to yer uncle or you nibbles when he's got Ol' Faithful in his hands."

Ethan was about to object, but Lauren was standing behind Uncle when he said that, and she put her index finger to her lip and shook her head. He didn't like that

Sissy was letting Uncle think wrong. Sissy knocked that creature out! If he'd done the same thing, he'd be mad at Uncle for taking credit for it.

Uncle put Ol' Faithful back in the wagon. "Kids, it was a long night, and I didn't get much sleep. Can you get breakfast together and pack up while I get a few winks? I'll just have a biscuit or two while we travel."

"Of course, Uncle." Lauren grabbed the milk bucket. Ethan nodded towards Uncle as well. *He sure does look tired. I hope he won't be too grumpy today.* Ethan followed Lauren's lead and began packing up their belongings.

The children worked quickly, but it still took over two hours. When they were done, they woke Uncle. He carefully tied the frame he was drying the cougar's hide to the back of the driver's seat. It looked almost like it was a sail on a ship. *That's scary! I bet that will keep the bad ones away.* Uncle got in the wagon, and much to Ethan's surprise, the day went by without a single grumble from Uncle.

***

At noon of their seventh day on the road, Uncle stopped them just before they crested a small knoll. "Kids, it's Loggerton over that there hill. When I was through here on the way down to get you, it was a pretty wild and unsavory place."

This was the last thing Lauren expected to hear after the bishop's assertion that Loggerton was so peaceful and accepting. But then she realized that everything the bishop had said was a lie. She let out a hushed "Oh."

"I want to keep you kids safe from any shenanigans going on down there," Uncle continued. "I'm gonna find a place to lock up the wagon and board the horses, then scout around a bit."

"That sounds like a good idea, so what do we need to do?" Lauren looked at the boys, and their eyes were glued on Uncle, so she knew they were listening.

Uncle got down from the wagon. "I need you three to just hide in the wagon while I do that. I want you to lay down in here while I cover it with the tarp."

Aiden shook his head, "I don't really like that idea. What if somebody finds us in here while you are scouting?"

"You got them magic weapons of yours, right?" Uncle pointed to where Aiden's sword was stashed.

Aiden did a double-take and paused. Lauren was just as shocked as he seemed to be. Something about how he said that sounded sarcastic, but she just couldn't respond. Before she could formulate her own response, Aiden interjected, "Oh, I guess you are right."

Uncle pointed a gigantic finger directly at Ethan, "I need you to be really, really quiet."

Ethan puffed up his chest and nodded. "I can do it, Coo Coo."

"All right, lie down." Uncle began to unroll the tarp on the side of the wagon.

"Wait, Uncle!" Aiden said as he scrounged around in a pack.

Uncle paused with his head cocked to one side. Aiden pulled the falcon hood out of the pack and put it on Daddy Duck. Lauren was amazed at Aiden's diligence in working with his pet. He had trained him to the point where he didn't need the hood to stay in the wagon. It was smart of him to put it on now, in case the duck didn't like being locked in under the tarp.

Aiden lay down next to Lauren, and Uncle proceeded to pull the tarp over the wagon. The wagon tilted slightly to one side, indicating Uncle had gotten back on, then leveled out before she could feel them moving toward Loggerton.

***

What Uncle didn't realize was they had already been discovered, but not by anyone he would expect. In the shadow of a large oak tree just off the side of the road, crouched a stealthy observer. From the road, the creature would have looked like a large rock encrusted with moss and lichen.

At the sight of Daddy Duck, the creature almost gave away its stealthy position in excitement. Looking at the golden duck, he was sure that if he could capture it, he could trade it to the evil man to free his bear. As the wagon proceeded on toward town, the creature carefully pulled the woven moss hood off of its head as it slowly stood up and looked for its next hidden observation point.

The creature raced as fast as its diminutive legs would take it from the large tree to a thicket of brush near the road and flattened to the ground to resemble an irregular patch of moss. With the cow slowing the wagon down, the creature was able to keep up.

When the wagon reached the edge of town, the creature grew anxious. It avoided the town whenever possible and then only went in at night if necessary. But the wagon pulled into the stable on the edge of town. The creature was relieved to be able to observe discretely from the woods.

The creature couldn't enter the stable from the front during the day, but there might be a back way, so it skirted around the barn in the woods, looking for a less-conspicuous entry point.

25. The Lost will be Found

The acolyte's accommodations the first night were in the stable loft. This left him free from notice to sneak out and make sure his horse and packs were unharmed.

The horse he'd now thought of as Patches had done a good job of mowing down all the grass around where he'd tied it up. He gave the horse an apple he stole from the kitchen.

Patches finished the apple and looked at him expectantly. "No, I don't have any more." The horse looked down, and he thought the moonlight was playing tricks on him because the horse seemed to be pouting. *I should bring you back to the inn.*

He'd realized that he couldn't retrieve the horse permanently and keep up his waylaid traveler routine. But it was good to have a horse nearby for a quick getaway.

He scrounged some rope from the stable and tied the horse up, so it could roam farther. Then he took some time to build a lean-to by starlight and put grain from the barn in a depression under the lean-to. He brought Patches over to show him the grain, and the horse began to lazily chomp at it. "OK, Patches, I'll be back in a day or two to check on you."

Just to be safe, he grabbed his pack, the saddle, and horse tack and stored it under a lean-to he made of downed pine branches. *If someone finds Patches, they may be in a*

163

hurry to run off with the horse and not notice the rest of my gear. At least I'll be able to sell the leather goods for traveling money if I must.

***

For the next two days, he worked diligently for the matron. The work was easier than what he was expected to do as an acolyte. The patrons in the inn didn't expect the level of perfection the bishop did and largely ignored him like he was just part of the furniture. What he assumed about the shaved head and robe appeared to be true.

His apparent invisibility allowed him to listen in on everything the townsfolk said. Mostly, they focused on the weather, the sawmill, and how glad they were that the Light had returned to the village.

This last point didn't make sense to him. He'd been here when the bishop came and brought the censers with the Ylohnu Light to the town. The night was alight with their red glow. *The whole town was far livelier than it is now. Why are they glad the true light is gone?*

He was frustrated with his mute act because he wanted to correct them for their foolish ways. But at the same time, they spit every time the bishop was mentioned. It was almost like his title was some kind of curse word. *I definitely want to know what that's all about before I break my cover.*

On his third day at the inn, after the last breakfast patron left, a young woman entered, wearing a long red gown that was frayed on the edges and covered in patches of burrs and thorns. It was tight-fitting around her body, and it split on either side, showing her legs, which had scratches on them. She wore muddy sandals of black leather that had straps that went up to her knees. She had shoulder-length flaming red hair that was tangled and had a few twigs stuck in it, and the red paint on her lips was faded and irregular. Even the polish on her fingernails was chipped. Her face was overall painted white, but her eye makeup was smeared and streaked like she'd been crying. She also had scratches on her face, arms, and legs, like you might get from thorns in the woods.

He recognized her as one of the entertainers the bishop recruited when he set up the pavilion in front of the church. The acolyte wasn't sure exactly what her act was, as she performed in an exclusive section of the pavilion. However, she seemed very popular and glamourous. He couldn't imagine how someone like her could end up so disheveled and beaten.

The matron stopped cold as she saw the woman. Then she dropped the tray she was holding and ran to the young woman. It crashed to the floor, spilling its contents everywhere. The acolyte used cleaning up the mess as an excuse to come closer and eavesdrop.

The woman in red sank to her knees and wept. "Mama, I'm so sorry! You were right. You were right."

The matron knelt next to her and held her tight, also weeping. "None of that now. You were lost and now are found. I missed you so much."

165

After a moment, the matron looked over her shoulder, "Dear boy, could you take that to the kitchen?"

Not wanting to damage his place with the matron, he exited the dining room and busied himself with the lunch dishes in the kitchen. He had time to finish the breakfast dishes before the matron called for some milk and bread. He brought them to her and the young woman.

The daughter sat at a table with her mother's arm around her shoulder. "The night the censers exploded, there was chaos in the camp. I really don't remember how I got shuffled out of town—only that at one point, a giant threw me over his shoulder and carried me across a stream."

The matron's eyes flew wide as her mouth gaped open, "A Heath Warden, in league with the Darkness? If the giants have turned, these are truly dark days."

The acolyte was disturbed by this discussion. The censers brought the true light. With them destroyed, of course, bad things were bound to happen. He wanted to confront this heresy once and for all but decided it could wait for the rest of the story to be told.

He stood there for a moment, expecting her to continue. But the matron looked up. "Go on now. Start getting ready for the lunch rush." *I need to know what happened.* The matron's upraised eyebrows and pursed lips showed him it was time to move along.

The daughter continued as he retreated to the kitchen, "A couple of days later, the bishop returned. He was furious, something about some children, and he went into a

166

rage yelling and screaming ….” she broke down crying as the door closed behind the acolyte.

That doesn't sound like the bishop. There's more to this story. I've got to hear it. He cracked the door and continued to listen as the daughter continued, “He had people in a cage! I knew I couldn't stay there.”

The Acolyte caught his breath. *People in a cage, what people in a cage? That doesn't sound like the bishop. They must have been heretics.*

The girl continued, “I woke early and convinced the guards I was going to the privy. I snuck out of the camp and into the woods. I was so scared.”

He heard more sobs before she continued, “I remembered how you used to say all rivers lead to Loggerton, So I found a stream and followed it. Eventually, I came to the back of the stables.”

There was a pause, and the acolyte couldn't tell what was happening. Then he heard a defiant, “Mother! We can't leave those people locked in a cage. I know where they are!”

“There will be time for that soon enough. We'll talk to the parson when he returns this afternoon.” There was a brief pause. “Darling girl, you have been through so much. Let's get you cleaned up.”

The matron called for the acolyte, and he paused for a moment before stepping out of the kitchen. “I'll be in the washroom for a bit," she said. "Mind the dining room for me. Knock if we have any customers."

The acolyte nodded and busied himself with picking up the half-eaten loaf of bread and mug of milk. The matron directed her daughter into the washroom. As the acolyte returned from the back room, an enormous man stepped into the dining room. The light in the doorway backlit his silhouette, and the acolyte couldn't get a clear picture of his face.

"You all have room in yer stable to lock up my wagon and horses?" the man asked, pointing over his shoulder.

The acolyte froze. *That's the big man from the church!* Outside, he saw a cougar pelt flying from the back of his wagon like a sail. *The cougar didn't work!*

He stared wide-eyed at the frontiersman. *It didn't even slow them down. The evil children must be here too.*

The big man snapped his fingers in the acolyte's face. "Did ya hear me? I need a secure place for my goods." The big man put his hands on his hips. "What's the matter? Cat got yer tongue?"

The acolyte nodded as he tried to formulate a plan. The girl's story told him how to find the bishop. *I must go upstream. If I leave soon, I bet I can follow her tracks.* If he could somehow stall the children here, the bishop could deal with them.

"Are you saying you have a room or that yer a mute?" the big man asked as his face turned red, and his mouth twisted into a scowl, barely visible under his bushy beard.

Thinking fast, the acolyte pointed inside and nodded his head. Then he covered his mouth with his hand and nodded again.

The big man sputtered. "Oh, sorry. Didn't mean to offend. Didn't realize you were mute."

The acolyte used the moment of confusion to seize the initiative. He pulled the stable key off its ring near the door and grabbed the big man's elbow to pull him back outside. The acolyte led him to the stable. *This could work to my advantage. Maybe I can lock him and the evil kids in here and burn the place down!*

After taking a brief tour of the stable, the frontiersman asked, "How much fer the whole place fer the night?"

The acolyte held up his hand with all five fingers splayed wide. "Five silvers, huh? A bit steep. That get me some vittles and a place to stay?"

The acolyte pointed to the loft. Then held up two fingers and pointed to the inn.

"Seven! That's highway robbery!" Uncle looked around the barn and then back at the acolyte. "All right, but I need a bunk room for four."

The acolyte tried acting surprised by the request by raising an eyebrow. He must have conveyed the right

169

emotion because the big man followed up, "You bein' a mute, and all this ought to go without sayin', but no questions asked."

No questions asked? This is going to be fun. The acolyte held out his hand the way he'd seen porters do for a tip.

The big man fished around in his pouch and pulled out a silver, and exclaimed, "Bah, gettin' hustled by a mute stable boy." He tossed the acolyte the silver just the same.

The acolyte pocketed the silver and handed the big man the stable key. They returned to the front of the inn, and the big man mounted his wagon as the acolyte went inside.

He didn't see the children but assumed they had to be hiding under the tarp of the wagon. *I wish the cougar had worked, but at least I know where they are. Now I just need to find the bishop.*

26. A Hole in the Barn

After Uncle led the horses into the barn, he peeked under the tarp to check on the kids. "You OK in there?"

The kids gave him a silent thumbs-up.

"When I close the door, you'll hear a loud bang from the bar on the outside. You can get out from under here and roll up the tarp, but don't leave the barn." Then he put the tarp back down.

As Uncle turned to leave, a hole in the barn caught his eye. *That hole ain't much bigger than Ethan, but sure enough, that boy might try to go explorin' on me. Then again, he's been a good kid so far. It might be better not to mention it to give him any ideas.*

He unhitched each of the horses and put them in their own stalls and then went out and locked the door, making sure to bang the bar loudly to signal the kids. That done, he proceeded to check out the town.

***

"That was it! That was the bar Uncle said he'd bang," Aiden whispered to Lauren as she rolled onto her hands and knees.

"You're right," Lauren said.

Aiden followed Uncle's directions and rolled up the tarp, and then checked on their animals, Lauren and Ethan

171

accompanying him. Meow Meow was his sleepy self, completely oblivious to the change in surroundings.

Aiden took a moment to survey the barn. Sunlight came in from several windows on the first floor and through big hay doors on the upper floor. His eye caught a glint of light off a water crock with tin cups hanging from it. He hopped down and took a drink.

Ethan watched from the wagon, "Aiden, I need some water for Sparkle Frog."

Oh, I'd better help Daddy Duck too. I almost forgot he had the hood on. Aiden handed the tin of water to Ethan and climbed back into the wagon.

Ethan poured the water into Sparkle Frog's bucket, and the frog let out a croak that resounded through the barn.

Aiden froze and listened intently for anyone who might decide to investigate. Lauren and Ethan must have had the same thought because they looked as still as statues. *I guess Uncle checked things out first to make sure no one was about.*

Aiden took Daddy Duck's hood off, and the duck immediately perked up and stretched its wings. Daddy Duck let out an alarmed quack and flew into the air as far as the cord would let it.

"What's got you spooked, Daddy Duck?" Aiden turned in the direction the duck was looking and, just inside a hole in the back of the barn, was a little gray creature with a spiny head wrapped up in what looked like a moss cloak.

"To Arms!" Aiden dove for his sword. "There's a demon!"

"Where?" Ethan's voice quivered as he sprang into action.

Lauren put a hand on Aiden's shoulder. "Wait! Look, he's acting like a toddler."

Aiden saw that the creature was focused on Daddy Duck. It had both arms out, and it was gently calling "quack" as if Aiden and his siblings weren't there at all.

Ethan had his shield now, and his brow was furrowed, "Sissy, I don't have any power."

Lauren shook her head, looking down at the shaft of her spear. "I don't either. I don't think he's a threat."

Aiden didn't feel threatened by the creature either. He hoped Lauren was right. The creature looked like it could be evil, with its unnatural skin and spiny head. *I guess there's no other way to find out.*

Aiden set his sword on the side of the wagon and hopped down in front of the creature. "Who are you?"

The creature froze, like a deer in the woods when it first sees a person. Aiden approached with his hands open, like how Daddy taught him to approach a wounded animal. In a flash, the creature flipped its hood up and dashed out of the hole in the barn.

Aiden bolted after it, but Lauren yelled, "Wait!"

173

Lauren pointed at their weapons. "It seems harmless, but we don't know what's going on in this town."

Aiden pulled up short as he reached the hole in the barn. Lauren had a point. But looking outside, he couldn't see the creature at all. He turned back to size up Ethan and then at the gap in the wall. *I know I can't make it out of this hole, and I'm not sure even Ethan could.*

"OK, Sissy, you're right." Aiden turned to Lauren. "But what do we do now?"

The creaking of hinges sounded behind them. "What do you do now about what?" Light cascaded into the barn from the front doors making Uncle a silhouette.

"There was a creature, Uncle." Ethan pointed at the hole in the barn. "It was all gray and spiky. It wore funny fur."

"A gray and furry creature, you say?" Uncle raised his right eyebrow. "Sounds like a badger or coon. I was worried about that hole in the barn."

Aiden's blood boiled at that. *We live in the woods! We know what a badger or a coon looks like. Why won't Uncle just believe us?*

Aiden was about to give Uncle a piece of his mind when Uncle lifted a fifty-pound feedbag onto his shoulder and started walking towards the hole in the wall.

"It was a lot darker in here before you opened the door," Lauren caught Aiden's eye and shook her head.

174

Again? *We're going to let Uncle think the wrong thing. I don't get it. I'm going to have to talk to her when he's not around.*

"I guess you're right, Sissy," Aiden felt bad about the deception. He really wanted to get things straight with Uncle about the Light and Darkness once and for all.

Ethan opened his mouth to respond, but Uncle cut him off, "Won't be no critters gettin' in here tonight."

He set the bag of feed down. Then picked up a small rectangular bale of straw and set it in front of the hole. Then he placed the feed bag on top of that.

Aiden admired how Uncle could just "fix" something if he wanted to. *That would stop me from getting in here . . . unless I ate straw. Wait, what would a creature like that eat?*

Uncle interrupted his musings. "Who wants a hot meal with fresh bread and butter?"

"Me! Me!" Ethan said, raising his hand. The other children nodded enthusiastically.

"Come along then. That matron at the inn needs a sack o' taters." Uncle turned to the wagon and threw Ethan over his shoulder, and started carrying him out of the barn.

"Coo Coo, you're funny." Ethan laughed hard and loud. It was the first time Aiden had heard that in a long time. *Maybe this won't be so bad after all.*

Lauren hopped down and followed Uncle out the door. Aiden trailed behind but then looked back at the bale of straw and wondered what exactly that creature was and if Uncle's contraption would really keep it out.

27. Respite

Ethan was the first out of the barn, with Lauren and Aiden quickly behind. He followed Uncle into the inn. Fresh bread would be so good. When they entered, the matron stepped from the washroom and started talking to somebody hooded in a white robe.

The matron looked at the group and frowned. "Now, what kind of man lets his children get so filthy?"

Oh, Uncle's not going to like that! Ethan looked up and saw Uncle's brow furrow. *He's getting mad. I can help.* "He's not our Daddy." Ethan shook his head and then pointed at Uncle. "He's our Coo Coo."

The matron burst out in laughter. "With that wild mountain man look he's got there, I'd say Coo Coo is about right." Ethan looked up and had to agree that she was right. Uncle did look wild.

"Hey now!" Uncle barked. "Do you make it a point to be disrespecting paying customers?"

"My apologies." The matron stepped back and squared her shoulders. "I just meant that the whole lot of you need a hot bath by the looks of it."

Uncle looked down at Ethan and then back at Lauren and Aiden. "Yeah, ain't that the truth."

The matron added a couple of logs to the fire to heat up the water. "We'll get you some food. Just have a seat where you like."

Ethan quickly climbed on to the bench at the nearest table. His siblings and Uncle followed him. The person in the robe left the room and returned with four tin cups and a pitcher of milk. Meanwhile, the matron went into the kitchen.

Ethan looked at the hooded figure, and something about his eyes reminded him of someone, but he couldn't remember who. "Don't I know you?"

The servant shook his head and quickly turned back, and rushed to the kitchen.

Ethan was about to call after him, but Uncle put a hand on his shoulder. "The boy can't speak; he's a mute."

"Oh," Ethan said with a look of concern on his face. "How did that happen, Coo Coo? Did the Dark One get him?"

"I don't know about no Dark One," Uncle replied with a pause as he drank some milk. "Sometimes people are born that way. Sometimes accidents happen. Regardless, it ain't polite pryin' into others' business."

Ethan could tell by Uncle's crinkled eyebrows that this was serious. "OK, Coo Coo. But he sure does seem familiar."

"It's OK, E," Aiden interjected, "He looks familiar to me too."

Lauren set her cup down. "I would say the same, but I know we have never met a mute person before."

"Happens sometimes," Uncle explained. "Especially when you get away from home. You start thinking you see people you know. People look a lot more alike than you think."

The Matron approached with a cutting board with sliced bread, ham, sausages, cheeses, pickles, and a mound of fresh butter. "Well, I don't travel far, but I'm always seeing people I think I've met before. Like you, weren't you in here just a week or so ago?"

"Yes, ma'am," Uncle replied. "Came through on my way to get these nibbles fer their summer trip to their granny's house. Seem to recall you had some mighty fine ale." Uncle shook his empty cup at her.

"That was before," The matron looked down at her feet. "We had some changes in these parts."

"Changes?" Uncle asked, raising an eyebrow. "I see the circus ain't in town, and you don't have those censers everywhere. What's that got to do with the ale?"

Just then, a girl in a white robe, like the boy servant, came out of a side room. Her hair was wet and combed straight with a part down the middle, but she had scratches on her face and arms. *Oh, that looks owie. Maybe Sparkle*

Frog can help. She scurried across the room and into the kitchen.

The matron turned back to Uncle. "My daughter will be speaking at church this evening and will tell you exactly what this has to do with ale."

Uncle investigated his empty mug. "I ain't exactly the goodness and light church type, ma'am."

"Maybe you should be," the matron retorted. "If more men sought the true Light, maybe this wouldn't have happened to my daughter."

Ethan hopped up and pulled on the matron's skirt. "She looks owie. Sparkle Frog makes head eggs go away." He patted the top of his head.

She looked down at Ethan with a broad smile on her face. "That's good to know, little one. But I'll take care of my own kin. Now you all eat your vittles, and when you're done, you'll get a bath and clean clothes."

The matron pointed out the door where the church could be seen. "Then you can be my guest at services tonight even if your uncle's not so inclined."

"Now, listen here. These nibbles are my kin." Uncle gave the matron a hard stare. "So, I'll be the one taking them to services."

"Very well." The matron responded flatly. "But if you're going to services, you'd best be cleaning behind those ears."

Ethan let out a belly laugh at that. Lauren and Aiden joined him.

The matron reached down and gave his ear a tug. "That means you too, little one," the matron said with a wink, then left the room.

They all sat in silence for a few moments, eating from the cutting board. The girl came back out and began tidying the room. Ethan could tell she was limping a bit, and she winced every now and then as she did things. *I should ask Uncle if I can get Sparkle Frog after church to help her.*

He wasn't sure what happened to the girl, but he guessed they would find out at services tonight. *But do I really want to know?*

28. A Return to Darkness

The acolyte kept a low profile while the big man and children were in the dining room. *I have them right where I want them, and they have no idea who I am.* With their wagon and horses in the stable, he could sabotage it and keep them here as long as he liked. Then he could sneak off and bring back the bishop and his forces.

I don't want to blow this; I need to play along . . . for now. He followed the matron's lead as she and her daughter readied themselves for church.

The big man and the children did likewise and cleaned up for services. As they were leaving, the matron's daughter stopped the girl for a moment and tied her hair with a light blue ribbon, and put a bonnet on her head. This made the little girl smile, and the two walked hand in hand reverently to the services. *Ugh, I can't stand that girl. A ribbon and a bonnet's not going to hide the stench of evil on her.*

The boys and the big man trailed behind them, literally dragging his feet, but it appeared that the man was more interested in keeping an eye on the children than attending services.

When they got to the church, the acolyte noticed a series of black divots in the earth. They appeared to be craters situated in a circle around where the pavilion used to be. *That's where the censers were. They must have exploded! What could have caused that?* His stomach clenched in a wave of dread. He knew the censers were powerful relics of a bygone age. Just a few days earlier, they cast the town in their light of true knowledge and enlightenment. *What happened here?* The whole town was streaming towards the church in the same reverent state as the girls. *How could they all have abandoned the true light so quickly?*

He entered the church and noticed it hadn't changed much. There were twenty rows of wooden benches on a rough hardwood floor. The front had a prayer rail with a pulpit on raised platforms with doors on either side. The platform had a four-feet square of new wood in it that hadn't been stained yet. *That's where the censer had been. It must have exploded as well!*

The matron and her daughter went into the door on the right, where the parson's office was, just like the Heathland's chapel. *Should I join them to see what tale they are sharing with the parson?*

As he stood there in indecision, the big man directed the children to take seats in the last row of the wooden benches. He stepped behind the children with his back to the wall. He took up the stance of a sentry with his eyes darting around the room. *I don't think he trusts what's going on here anymore than I do. Can I use that somehow?*

The acolyte stepped forward to see if he could spy on the conversation with the parson, but the matron and her daughter came out of the office and sat down on the empty front bench. He quickly took a seat on one of the empty benches in the back as the parson, wearing the same simple white clothes as everyone else, stepped up to the pulpit. "Dearly beloved, let us pray now for the return of Loggerton to the Light." The parson bowed his head and began a prayer.

The acolyte bowed his head, but he wasn't praying along. *What? They had the light of knowledge, and it's gone!* The acolyte remembered all his training in the rituals of the Y'lohnu Light, and none of them started off like this. He wanted to scream, *"This isn't how a proper service goes at all!"*

The parson completed his prayer. "Amen, brothers and sisters. On Wednesday, we normally have an extended time of praise and prayer." He pointed down to the front row. "However, tonight, our lost sister has been found. She has a testimony to share. As a congregation, we are to discuss how we complete purging the Darkness from Loggerton."

There was a chorus of "amen" and "hear, hear" from the audience at this forceful decree. This made the acolyte's blood boil; he could feel the heat rising up his neck. He wondered if the big man was in line with everyone else and turned to see the frontiersman had stopped scanning the crowd and was now riveted on the parson.

The parson continued, "I have to warn you, brothers and sisters, that this testimony is not for the faint of heart and best not for the young ones. She has a tale of the evil forces that were at work in our very town just a few days ago."

He pointed to the left side of the church as he spoke, "Mrs. Miller and Mrs. Cobbler, would you mind having a children's time out of doors on this nice evening?" The two young mothers got up with their children in hand and went out of the church.

The acolyte continued to watch the frontiersman to see how he would handle this. The big man ran his hand down his beard. Then he motioned for the children to go on with the women. But for some unknowable reason, he decided to sit down. *He must be one of them, after all. It's the only reason he'd stay for this charade.*

As the last child left, he realized they were only being looked over by a couple of young mothers. *Could I take them now? They are unarmed.*

He mulled this over for a few seconds but quickly decided against it as he had no weapons himself or a real plan to spirit them away. *Maybe I can pull something off at the end of the service. Oh, I'm supposed to meet with the parson then.* With the matron's daughter arriving, his help at the inn might not be needed. The Matron might put him in the parson's care, and it would be even harder to get away. *If I'm going to go find the bishop, I need to go now!*

As the last children filtered out of the service, he took his leave as well. The children turned to the grassy area to the right as they exited the church, so he turned to the left and darted to the cover of the nearest building. After checking for pursuit that didn't come, he continued to the inn via back alleys. When he got there, he climbed into an open kitchen window, grabbed an empty flour sack from the pantry, and filled it with cheese and sausages.

He needed to sabotage the big man's wagon if he could. He realized too late that the only keys to the stable were with the matron and the big man. *There's a hole in the back of the stable. Maybe I can get in there.* He ran to the back and found it blocked with a bale of straw. He kicked it, and it didn't move. *The big man's more clever than I thought.*

It was more important to get to the bishop quickly than it was to sabotage the wagon, so he rushed through the woods at top speed to find Patches lazily munching grass. He quickly re-outfitted Patches for traveling and grabbed his pack.

He felt a pang of guilt as he dropped the matron's robe in the dirt to put on his acolyte robe. *She had been kind, but she's not one of us.* He threw his pack on Patches' back and led the horse upstream. Both of them stomped the robe into the ground in the process.

The matron's daughter had said she'd followed the water downstream. *I need to find some trace of her to know if she came down a side stream instead of the main.* He took a game path near the stream, and the trek became slow going as he tried to verify he was going the right way. He scanned the ground for a sign of where to go and eventually found human footprints in the soft earth heading towards town. He was no expert tracker, but she clearly wasn't trying to hide her path very well.

At the second feeder creek, he found torn cloth that looked like it matched her dress. A quick look identified footprints he could follow farther upstream. In the failing light, he realized he should have brought a torch. *I'm going to lose her trail in the dark.*

On multiple occasions, he retraced his steps to work around a briar patch or fallen trees that were impassable by the horse. By the time he realized that the horse had caused him three or four hours backtracking, he was ready to let it loose. He let out a deep sigh. *I need something to show the bishop my story is true. The parson's horse has to be worth a lot. But this is wasting so much time.* As he was about to give up altogether, he noticed a vague reddish light in the distance.

He found a game path that seemed to be going in that general direction, and as he got closer, the path widened, seeming to be regularly used by people. Near midnight, he broke out of the woods and into a clearing with the pavilion the bishop had brought to Loggerton. *I'm home! But will he accept me after the failure with the children?*

29.Darkness Revealed

Lauren watched as Uncle came out of the church with the rest of the adults. His brow was furrowed, and he had a deep frown like he'd heard something devastating. Lauren and the boys ran and followed him as he headed for the Inn.

Lauren took Uncle's hand and looked up at him, "Uncle, what's wrong?"

"I don't get all caught up in this Dark and Light stuff, but what was goin' on here was just plain wrong." Uncle shook his head.

Lauren's eyes went wide at this. Loggerton seemed like a really nice place. Everyone was so kind. "What do you mean, Uncle?"

"They had you nibbles leave fer a reason. It's nothin' to be spoken about to you young'uns," Uncle replied as he patted Lauren on her shoulder. "I knew somethin' was off about this place on my way through." Uncle paused and shook his head. "Never seen a church attached to a circus tent. Didn't stay long enough when I passed through here to find out what was going on."

Aiden came closer and took Uncle's other hand. "What happened to it?"

Uncle didn't respond right away. "I guess yer gonna keep askin' till you get something you can understand." He let out a deep breath, "The parson said the bishop had this place lit up with a bunch of red glowing censers. As he tells it, a few days ago, in the middle of the night, the censers all exploded and knocked down the tent." Uncle turned back toward the church and pointed at the divots on the ground. "All the unsavory types causing all the trouble loaded up the tent and were gone by morning."

Aiden let go of Uncle's hand and began to look around the town. "Where did they go?"

"Nobody was fer sure until the matron's daughter came home today." Uncle pointed towards the stream. "They are a couple of miles upstream, hiding out in the woods."

Uncle increased his pace slightly and urged the children on. "The town's apparently up in arms about the whole deal and are planning to drive them out of the area. Apparently, they have some people locked up in cages."

"People locked up in cages?" Aiden asked. "What people? Father and Mother?"

Uncle shook his head, "They didn't say who. But regardless, we need to be long gone before the ruckus starts."

Ethan ran in front of Uncle and started walking backward. "But if it's Mama and Daddy. We can help!"

"Yeah! Daddy left us weapons to fight the Darkness," Aiden chimed in. "I think the censer we destroyed must have been connected to the ones here."

Uncle stopped in his tracks and looked at them a little less skeptically than usual. "They didn't say who, but this is

189

a long way off from where yer Ma went looking fer yer Pa. Can't think that's who they'd have locked up here."

Ethan stopped and held up a hand palm out, "But couldn't we go be a sneaky spy and see if it's Mama and Daddy?"

Uncle just kept walking and picked Ethan up in his right arm. "All you nibbles might be brave in the face of fighting off some wild animal like that sick cougar. Trying to scout out an enemy camp and not be seen is something else." He shook his head. "Yer gran would tan my hide fer even entertaining the idea of letting you get caught up in this kind of fight. Regardless of how bad these people are."

He looked down at Aiden, "If word gets back to them bad ones before the town is ready, they might stage a sneak attack, and they have a giant!"

A Heath Warden turned to the Darkness! Lauren tensed as a chill ran down her spine, "That would be bad! Is it too late in the day to leave?"

"Yeah, but we should be ready to skedaddle if there's trouble." Uncle stepped up his pace as he continued to the inn.

Aiden pulled on Uncle's free hand and looked up at him with big eyes, "But Uncle, you're big and strong, and we have our weapons. We can scout and see if it is Mama and Daddy."

"It's supposed to be rough country between here and there, and we'd be casting about in the dark trying to find the place without a guide." Uncle looked down at Aiden and shook his head, "Most likely, we'd just stumble into their camp and set off the alarm. That giant would be on us with no way to outrun him." Uncle pulled his hand away from Aiden and pointed his index finger at him. "Ain't no way I'm puttin' you all in that kind of danger, no how."

Aiden bowed his head. "OK, Uncle."

Lauren felt bad for Aiden because of Uncle's rebuke. But she agreed with him and felt compelled to let the boys know it. "Uncle's right. We can't just wander blindly through the woods into danger."

Uncle picked up his pace, "That's more like it. We need to hurry up and get ready to leave first thing while there's still light."

Aiden ran after. "Why don't we sleep in the barn with the wagon," Aiden offered.

That was a quick turnaround. Lauren wondered if he was still thinking about how to capture the little creature that wanted Daddy Duck, or worse, sneaking out to scout anyway.

"That'd be fine fer you nibbles, but not for me. Not enough room." Uncle put his arms out wide to emphasize his size.

Aiden pressed the conversation. "You could sleep in the inn, and we'd be safe in the stable."

They all stepped up onto the porch of the inn. Lauren looked down at her brother with furrowed eyebrows. *What is Aiden up to? I really don't want to sleep in the stable. This is the last time we'll get a chance to sleep in a bed.*

Before she could provide an argument, Aiden continued, "If trouble doesn't come, you get a good night's sleep, and you can just take off as soon as you wake up."

Ethan piped up, "Yeah, you don't even have to wake us up. You can just take off." Ethan caught Lauren's eye and gave her a big wink.

Now Ethan's in on it too. Why on earth would the boys want to sleep in the back of the wagon instead of a real bed?

Uncle looked off toward the setting sun and stroked his beard. "All right, sounds good. I'll get the matron to fix some vittles for the road and will be up first thing."

They entered the dining room and sat down. Lauren expected the mute boy to serve them. She hated that she didn't know what the boys were up to. But it wouldn't do to ask them with Uncle at the table.

Ten minutes later, the matron's daughter came and served them. The mute boy was nowhere to be found. *He sure seemed familiar. Maybe Uncle was right about seeing people's twins out on the road.*

***

Under Uncle's direction, the children nestled into the wagon, making sure Meow Meow, Daddy Duck, and Sparkle Frog were fed and happy. Uncle locked the stable and went into the inn for the night.

Lauren heard Aiden whispering numbers under his breath. It sounded like he was counting down from one hundred.

"Three, two, one." Aiden jumped up and headed for the back of the wagon. The light was fading fast; everything Lauren could see was a muted orange.

Lauren sat up. "Aiden, what are you doing?"

"I have a hunch that creature will be back." Aiden hopped out of the wagon.

"Me too. I don't want it to eat the straw and come get Sparkle Frog." Ethan scurried after Aiden.

Lauren chuckled at Ethan's lack of proportion. *A little creature like that couldn't eat a whole straw bale.* Just the same, they'd seen some incredible things.

"If that's what you were thinking, why didn't you tell Uncle?" Lauren crawled out of the wagon to get a better look at what he was doing.

Aiden grabbed an empty feed bag, then untied the one on the straw bale blocking the hole in the wall. "You know he didn't believe us." Aiden pushed on the open sack and dumped about half the feed into the empty bag.

He had a point. Still, this seemed dishonest. How would it affect the Light?

Aiden tried pulling on the bag on the bale, and it slowly slid free and off to the side. It dropped with a thump on the bag he had been filling with grain.

Aiden pushed the straw bale so it made a corridor for entry into the barn from the hole. Finally, Aiden climbed up to the hayloft and hung a rope from a rafter, then climbed down and tied one end to the bag. *Where did he find that rope?* It always amazed Lauren how Aiden could put his inventions together from out of nowhere.

This looked like what Aiden described as the trap they used in the Tower of Light. "Are you going to knock that poor little guy out like you did to Knight Protector? He looked like he was just a baby."

Aiden began making a loop with a slip knot on the end that wasn't tied to the bag. "No, his head was pointy. It looked like he might be hard-headed."

Ethan knocked his fist on the top of his own head, "Yeah, those spiky things would make it hard to conk his wonkus."

Aiden nodded. "But he's little, so I think this should work to catch him and pull him off the ground far enough so he can't get away." He continued to set the trap. "I want to know why he was so interested in Daddy Duck. He didn't seem evil, so if he's tied up, we should be able to ask him safely."

"I don't think he's evil either," Lauren looked off into the growing darkness at the back of the barn. "He seemed more like Ethan when he was three, and somebody else had his blankey."

Aiden finished his trap. "Yeah, I got that impression too."

Ethan cocked his head. "How could Daddy Duck be his blankey?"

"Daddy Duck's not his blankey. I can't really explain it." Lauren paused for a minute, searching for the right word. "The creature just needed Aiden's friend. Like really bad."

Aiden's nod was hard to see as the light continued to dim outside. "Yeah, that's what I was thinking too."

"OK, boys, we need to get to bed before we can't see anymore." Lauren climbed up the wagon wheel into the wagon. The boys followed, and they all snuggled down in the blankets. *I hope we're right about this, and it's not really a dangerous minion of Darkness.*

***

About an hour later, a pair of close-set eyes looked through the hole in the barn to see if its quarry was still there. Starlight filtered into the barn from cracks between the boards, and the creature could barely make out the mass of the golden duck nestled in the wagon.

Something was different about the hole. In the pale starlight, he couldn't really make it out, but something wasn't right. Its intuition told him to run, but the love for its bear pushed it forward. As it crept forward ever so carefully, it started to quietly try to get to the duck's attention by calling to it. "Quack, quack, QUACK." A rope trap wrapped around its leg and whipped it into the air.

The creature immediately began to cry. "No, no, no" From where he hung upside down, the humanoid saw the three little humans from earlier sit up in the wagon. "Pweeze, bad man, pweeze no hurt Tok. No hurt, Tok. Pweeze."

A light began to glow from the side of the wagon, but Tok couldn't see what caused it. He saw the three humans get down from the cart. *Did the bad man send them? He likes to trick me.* They treaded warily to where he was hanging upside down at their eye level.

"Hey, little guy," the biggest one approached first. "We're not going to hurt you. We just want to talk to you."

This confused Tok. *Bis'hops people just beat Tok. Why friendly talk?* In the pale light, he determined that it was a female human. They would call her a girl. *The Bis Hops girls could be nice. Maybe this one is nice.* It calmed down and stopped flailing.

The smallest one pointed at its chest. "I'm Ethan."

"Me Tok," it replied, mimicking the hand gesture. "E'Tan, Tok down?" He pointed at Ethan, then himself, then the ground.

The middle-sized one grabbed the rope holding Tok. "I'm Aiden. I can let you down, but you have to tell us why you came to get Daddy Duck. Deal?"

"Da Dee Duck?" Tok asked, clearly not understanding.

Lauren pointed at the sleeping duck. "Why did you come for Quack?"

"Quack? Tok down. Tok tell," the creature said as it nodded its head.

"Tok down." Aiden picked the feed bag up to his chest. Tok began to slowly descend and ended up with his back on the ground and one leg still in the air. "Tok tell and be quick about it. This thing is heavy."

"Bad man has Bear," Tok explained. "Tok get Quack. Trade Quack for Bear."

"Bad man?" Aiden asked, grunting from the effort of holding the bag. "What bad man?"

"Bis'hop," Tok spat. "Bad man."

Tok felt the rope tighten on his leg as he saw Aiden stagger as if from a blow at the name of the bad man.

"The bishop!" Lauren exclaimed. "He's our enemy too. Aiden, let him go."

"OK, Lauren." Aiden lifted the sack over his head, and Lauren untied Tok's leg. "Tok, do you know where the bad man is?"

"Up water." Tok pointed outside.

"I think he means upstream, like the girl's story." Aiden offered.

Lauren nodded. "How far?"

"Not far. Tok fast. Give Quack?" Tok held out his arms, expecting the children to give him the duck.

"No, Tok, but we can help you save your bear." Lauren grabbed the staff of her spear from the side of the wagon. Blue-green light glowed from the tip.

Tok's eyes went wide at the light. *Sooo pretty, La'Ren must be angel.* "Ohhh." A note of awe escaped his lips.

Aiden took down a sword, and it erupted into flame. Tok stepped back away. Aiden said, "Wait, Tok. Don't be scared. We get the Light to fight the bad ones."

Tok was overwhelmed with awe. These children had power. He bowed down before them. Ethan came and tried to pull him up by the arm. "You don't need to do that. We're friends."

Tok reluctantly stood. He didn't know how to behave before these powerful people.

"We all have the Light," Ethan exclaimed. "God must want us to help Tok."

"We just need to get Uncle," Lauren squared her shoulders and held the spear in both hands.

"Save Bear!" Tok cried as he held his hand folded before him. "Pweeze!"

"But Uncle said he didn't think we could do a scout without being seen." Aiden edged toward the hole in the barn."

"No, Uncle was worried that if we didn't have a guide, we'd get caught." She pointed her spear at Tok. "We have a guide. I think he'll go on a scout with us."

Aiden shook his head, "Tok says the place is nearby. We can be sneaky. If it looks too dangerous, we can come get Uncle. If we ask for his help, he might just keep us locked up here, and poor Tok won't be able to get his bear."

"Yeah, Uncle never believes us, Sissy." Ethan jutted out his chin, "You beat that cougar, and he said he did."

Lauren slowly lowered her spear, shaking her head. "He told us he wouldn't even take us to spy things out. It feels dishonest to just go without telling him."

Tok's eyes filled with tears. *Would the girl not help now? She had to help!* "Save Bear?" Ethan ran up and hugged Tok. This made him feel better. Maybe the little one would help him.

The little boy turned to look at Lauren. "Sissy, the bishop is of the Darkness, not us. It might be Mama and Daddy in the cage. We need to help Tok and see who's in the cage!"

Lauren shook her head, "I guess Uncle did say he didn't want to be wandering without a guide. We have a guide, so I guess we can do a quick scout." She pointed her spear at Aiden. "But if we're seen, we need to run away immediately, ok!"

"Tok know sneaky way," the creature pointed out the hole in the barn, "No see."

"Yah, sissy, nobody will see us." Ethan crouched down, "We'll be sneaky spies."

Lauren walked to the hole in the wall, "Now, how are we going to get out of here?" she sighed. Tok realized the hole in the wall was much too small for La'ren or A'den to get out. *How were they going to get out?*

As if in answer, the flame on Aiden's sword intensified. "I think I can make the hole just a bit bigger, and we can get out."

Tok cowered away from the flame. *A'den has power!*

Aiden cut the hole a little wider, so it was almost the size of the straw bale. Despite the flames, the wall didn't catch fire. The sword just left the wood scorched at the hole's edges. Now they all fit through.

Once outside, Aiden said, "Show us the way Tok."

And the four of them crept off into the shadows with Ethan's shield lighting their way.

Tok hoped his new friends would be powerful enough to save Bear.

Still Small Voice

30.Growing Pains

The acolyte approached the camp warily. *Will I be remembered? Will they accept me?* As the horse crossed the threshold into the clearing behind him, he began to make out faint music coming from the pavilion.

The pavilion doesn't seem as grand. Something horrible happened for sure. Only two censers were providing the deep-red light of truth—one on either side of the tent entrance—rather than a censer every few feet surrounding the tent.

A low growl from his left startled him. The foliage and low light had hidden the bear cage. A shiver went down his spine. *Glad it's caged up. That beast would tear us apart if it got loose. I don't think it appreciates the bishop parading around its Bjorn Born in clown face and poking it with a spear.* As he continued to the pavilion, he was able to make out the other cages with various beasts used in the shows.

He approached the tent and found the two guards passed out by their posts. There was a bottle spilled on the ground, and he could smell the sickly rotten smell of wine. *Uggh! What is wrong with these men? Have they completely abandoned the light of truth?*

This gave him pause, and he took a tentative step back. Things aren't as I remember. The girl fled this place. Maybe she was right. Should I do the same?

Before he could act on his doubts, a slurred voice came from the ground. "Who goesh dere?" The guard on the left got on a knee with the help of his spear shaft.

There is no path but the Y'lohnu Light. I must go on. The acolyte straightened his back and put his fists on his hips. "I am the bishop's Acolyte of the Dandelion Order, and I bring him news from Loggerton and an offering."

"Yous kin give it to me, an I'll tell his holynesh," the guard slurred.

How do I get past this guy? What would the bishop do? "No!" The acolyte pointed an accusing finger at the guard. "A derelict such as yourself has no place in this holy rite. Take me to him. This is for him alone."

"No need to get yer robe in a twist." The guard stood up on wobbly legs. "I'll tell him and see."

"I'll tell him myself," the acolyte said as he stepped to the tent flap.

The guard turned the spear on the acolyte. "I don't care who you thinks you ish, boy. Nobody goesh in without his Holynesh clearin' it. Stay here."

The guard kicked his partner, who woke up and wobbled to his knees. Then one guard went inside. He was gone long enough that the acolyte thought he must have passed out before giving the message. The acolyte eased toward the tent flap only to be pushed back as the largest person he had ever seen strode out.

The man was literally a giant. He had to be nine feet tall. His thighs were as big around as the acolyte's waist. The acolyte took a step back to take in the enormity of the deer-hide-clad behemoth.

"What news do you bring?" the giant's frown highlighted a scar down his right cheek to his hard-chiseled chin. His hair was white, but he lacked the wrinkles of old age.

The thought of the giant rebuking him with a ham-fisted backhand broke the acolyte's earlier imperious act. "Loggerton knows where you are, and I think they are organizing an attack!"

"Bah. That's not news to bother His Holiness. You don't know your place, boy." The giant put his hand out. "What gift do you bring."

His Holiness, if he respects the bishop's authority, should respect me too. I am an Acolyte of the Dandelion Order, after all. He took a deep breath, "The gift is for the bishop himself. Not his lackeys. You are not of the orders; you have no right to demand anything of me."

"Lackey?" The giant raised his hand as if to strike the acolyte. *I can't show weakness. If the blow comes, I just must take it.* A tense moment passed as the giant looked down at him. Then without a word, the giant relented and went inside.

"Who dares interrupt my revels?" The bishop bellowed as he stepped out of the tent with his blood-red robes flowing around him.

The guards attempted to straighten up as the giant joined them. The bishop inspected the acolyte until a flicker of recognition crossed his face. "You survived? That is no great gift, given your pathetic performance at the tower." The bishop started pacing around the acolyte and his horse, acting like it was an inspection. "You couldn't even defeat three small children." He pointed an accusing finger in the acolyte's face. "And to think I entrusted you with the Y'lohnu globes to prepare you to attain the Order of the Rose Robes?"

The acolyte's cheeks flushed. *Now is not the time for weakness. He is right, I was defeated, but I won't be again.* "Your Holiness, I bring gifts. First, this horse I stole from the parson in the Heathlands."

"Bah, you'll have to do better than that." He waved a dismissive hand at the acolyte and turned to the tent.

"I have more." The acolyte pulled the cases with the writ for the children from his pack. "The evil children are in Loggerton now, and they are destined for Fairfields with a single man as their guardian."

The bishop paused and looked up at the giant. "This young acolyte may be worth something, after all."

The giant merely nodded, frowning.

"These writs give you the right to 'redirect' them to Blooming Glen as written, but I also know how to alter them further if you like." The acolyte handed the cases to the bishop.

205

"These are a good backup plan." The bishop took the cases. "But if you say there is but one man, Skull Crusher here should be sufficient to deal with him and the children." The giant slammed his enormous fist into his palm as the bishop continued, "Has my wayward apprentice brought me anything else of interest?"

The acolyte reached into the pack and pulled out the Horn of Power, then dropped to one knee and held it up to the bishop. Surely this should win his favor. "I return to you the Horn of Power that you might re-establish our power in this land."

The red light from the censers reflected in the bishop's eyes, and he wore a clear look of elation. "Oh, that is truly a mighty gift worthy of interrupting any revels."

The acolyte bowed his head in acknowledgment.

The bishop took the outstretched offering and inspected it. "You have returned one of our most powerful totems. I thought it might be lost for good to those evil children." The bishop touched the youth's right shoulder. "You truly are worthy of the Rose Robes."

I've done it! I've made it to the next level. A smile of satisfaction crossed the youth's face, but he kept his head down and waited for the bishop to continue. "Rise, you have done well."

The acolyte stood and looked the bishop in the eye as his mentor continued, "I am tempted to use this right now and storm Loggerton to wipe out the evil children and the whole town of unbelievers, but . . . that is mere vengeance talking."

The acolyte's jaw dropped. "What could be more important than stopping the evil children and making a lesson out of the unbelievers?"

"Our master has informed me of a strategic need in the Iron Hills." The bishop pointed to the south. "But for this, you must become a hero of legend, the binder of the Horn of Power. Do you still have the Ylohnu Globes?"

"Yes, Your Holiness, three." The acolyte was concerned he might be questioned about the two he'd used.

"That is more than enough." The bishop pointed to a censer. "Skull Crusher, a censer."

The giant stepped inside, leaving them quiet for an awkward moment. Then he returned with a harness and attached it to the censer, and then hoisted it onto his back.

The bishop led them to the cage with the bear. "My dear boy, you are about to take a step into a much larger world." The bishop put an arm around the acolyte. "The Iron Priestesses hold persistent sway over the people of the Iron Hills."

I really have done it. The bishop had never acted like this before. The acolyte looked at his mentor as the older man continued, "Our light of knowledge cannot hold sway there until they are unseated." The bishop held up the Horn of Power. "They stole their leadership from Refi'cul centuries ago and will not cede that power unless someone greater than them takes it."

The bishop motioned for Skull Crusher to put the censer down outside the cage with the bear. "Their sacred law states, 'With the Horn of Power, the mark of leadership, and a transformation of iron, the new leader shall rise.' With my help, you will become Refi'cul reborn." He blew smoke from the censer into the bear's face. It immediately dropped unconscious.

The bishop hung the horn around the acolyte's neck and placed his hands on the acolyte's shoulders. "Now, my young acolyte, are you willing to endure any pain for our cause?"

There's nothing he could do to me now that's worse than what I've already endured this past week. "Of course, Your Holiness."

The bishop stared into his servant's eyes. "Are you willing to follow my instructions without deviation or delay?"

With all I've been through to get here, he still doubts me. The acolyte nodded. "Yes, Your Holiness." *I will not fail.*

The bishop released the acolyte's shoulders, "Step to the bars and crouch with your face next to them."

What is this all about? Does he want me to take control of the bear-like I did the cougar? The acolyte took a knee as close to the cage as possible and put his face between the bars.

The bishop called to the bear, "Beast! Slash the boy's face and sleep."

What! No! The acolyte flinched back as the bear slashed his face open, leaving four claw marks down his cheek. The acolyte felt a scream well in his chest, and he clenched his teeth to silence it. Blood welled up from the cuts and rolled down his neck. The flinch was the only thing that kept the wounds from cutting deep into the muscle.

"Cauterize the wounds," The bishop demanded.

The acolyte rocked back on his knees. From the corner of his eye, he saw the giant jam a knife into one of the slots where smoke and light we're coming out of the censer.

It took all the acolyte had to maintain an upright position as he tried to use pressure from his palm on his cheek to stop the bleeding. *I was wrong. This is so much worse than the rest of the week. Had that girl been right to flee?*

The giant pulled out the blade, and it glowed red hot. *Can't scream, can't show weakness.* The giant held the blade against the slash closest to his ear, and the acolyte nearly passed out from the pain.

He sagged to his side, no longer able to hold himself up under the agonizing onslaught. *Will this ever end?*

Skull Crusher took a knee to finish the grisly task. Then he removed a flask from his belt and poured a foul-smelling liquid over the burned flesh. It felt like his entire face was on fire. In an act of sheer will, the acolyte gritted his teeth and rolled to his knees. Tears now flowed down his face, but he had not uttered a word during the ordeal.

"This one is tough, Your Holiness," the giant boomed as it wiped the blade on the ground near the acolyte's knees.

"Indeed. Heat the knife again." The bishop ordered.

What new hell am I to endure? Haven't I taken enough punishment? Despite the feeling of hopelessness, the acolyte resolved to take whatever came next. He gritted his teeth and placed his hands crossed in his lap.

The bishop motioned to the giant to give him the red-hot knife. The bishop reached through the bars and cut off a single claw from the bear. Under the influence of the censer's smoke, the bear didn't even flinch.

"This was necessary." The bishop helped the acolyte stand. "The cuts mark you as one who fought a bear and lived."

The bishop placed the bloody claw in the acolyte's hand. *Is that my blood or the bear's? Probably both.*

"This claw proves it was a bear and not something else. No one will question it." The bishop grabbed the acolyte's chin firmly and turned his head to inspect the wounds.

The acolyte used the last of his will power to remain standing while the bishop spoke. "You'll heal soon enough. This mark and the claw will give you the right to drink from the pool of strength in the Iron Mountains." The bishop turned his student to face the pavilion. "The Iron Priestesses maintain that no man can, which is why they rule."

The bishop patted him on the back. "You, my young apprentice, will usurp that rule."

Me? Rule the Iron Hills? The bishop does trust me! The revelation banished all the acolyte's previous doubts. "As you say, so it shall be, my master."

The bishop put a hand on the acolyte's shoulders. "Come with me to the tent for some brief revels. Then you must leave tonight while the Light is at its weakest."

Despite the excruciating pain in his face, the thought of leaving the area without vengeance on the evil children for putting him in this position frustrated him. "Master, what about the evil children? They were due to leave first thing in the morning."

The bishop turned. "My young acolyte has given me an excellent idea. Skull Crusher, take the censer, and go north now. Corrupt the local militia and cut off passage over the river. When you find a man and three children looking for a passage to Fairfields. Kill them."

"Yes, Your Holiness." The giant put on the harness and censer and left in a sprint to the north.

The bishop went to the cage and whispered something to the bear. Then he returned to the acolyte and put his arm around the youth's shoulder, directing him to the tent. Knowing the evil children would soon be getting theirs was going to make whatever diversions were in the tent so much sweeter.

Ethan followed Tok, lighting the way with his shield, and Aiden stayed close behind, with Lauren bringing up the rear. The word *consequences* floated in and out of her mind. As she started to imagine what those might be, she had to refocus on the woods to continue moving silently.

Tok clearly knew where he was going and took them down obscure game trails that had to be shortcuts through the underbrush. Within an hour, they saw a red haze in the distance. As they drew nearer, they slowed, and Tok motioned to stop and get down. He whispered, "Tok, look, you stay."

Lauren nodded, and the boys did as well. Tok scrambled through the underbrush and out of sight.

"Boys, this is just a scout, like Aiden said." Lauren hissed. It was bad enough that they were out of the barn without permission. They could end up in a fight and maybe get hurt.

"OK, Sissy, just a scout." Aiden nodded, and Ethan followed suit.

"Good. For now, we'll just keep quiet and see what Tok says." Lauren felt a little off-balance, so she planted her spear butt on the ground to lean against.

What seemed like an eternity later, Tok came back crying and trying very hard not to make any noise. "Bad man hurt Bear. Tok too scared to help. Bad Tok."

213

"Tok, you're not bad. The bad man is powerful. But we beat him before. Show us." Aiden stood up and took his sword in both hands.

Tok shot back through the brush with Aiden and Ethan in tow. "This is just a scout," Lauren hissed after the boys as she raced to catch up.

Tok guided them around the perimeter of the camp. As they navigated the brush, they saw a red light move off to the north, and the light in the camp dimmed significantly. *Will our light give us away?* She tried peering through breaks in the brush but couldn't see anyone.

Tok slowed and broke through the brush. As Lauren caught up, she realized there was a cage with a sleeping bear in front of them.

In the distance, they saw a powerful-looking man in red robes with black hair. His arm was around a youth with a shaved head in yellow robes, and they walked toward a circus tent.

Aiden looked up at Lauren with wide eyes. "Sissy, that's the mute boy from the inn. He's a yellow acolyte!"

"That has to be the bishop." Lauren pointed with her spear. "What's that hanging at the acolyte's side?"

Aiden's mouth dropped open. "That's the Horn of Power!"

"How did they get it back?" Lauren looked wide-eyed at the boys. "Knight Protector took it to the parson."

"I hope something bad hasn't happened to the parson," Ethan frowned.

Aiden looked to the southwest and could see a faint light in the night sky. "The light's still shining. Maybe there's more than one horn."

"Yeah, that could be right." Ethan nodded. "Should we get help?"

Lauren paused in thought. Uncle was already going to be angry at them for sneaking out. To get caught up in a fight would be worse.

"Bear hurt!" Tok pulled on Lauren's arm. "Pweez, help!"

"Sissy, please!" Ethan pleaded.

Aiden pointed toward the tent. "They just went into the tent, and those guards aren't really paying attention. I think we can get the bear out if we're careful."

Before any discussion could occur, Tok scurried around to the front of the cage, and the boys followed. Tok squeezed through a set of bars by the door that was just slightly wider than the rest.

Lauren followed them around the cage and looked at the tent. The guards weren't guarding anything. *We can do this. We just must be quick.* She turned back to see Tok give the bear a big hug. *Awww, that's so cute.*

The bear opened its eye and then slammed Tok across the cage. The little creature crumpled into a ball on the far side of the cage. *Oh No! Tok!*

To her horror, Ethan squeezed through the bars and got between the bear and Tok. He slammed his shield down, and it expanded to a full-sized tower shield, blocking Tok from the view of the bear. The shield shone so brightly that the bear shrank back from the light.

"Sissy! Spear!" Aiden called as he lifted his flaming sword to strike the lock. Lauren threw her spear, and it caught the bear in its side.

The bear immediately dropped, but the spear returned to her hand, and she knew there must be more danger. She turned around and saw the two guards making their way toward them on wobbly legs.

"E! Check on Tok," Lauren called as she turned to face the new threat. "We have to get out of here!" She ran off to face their attackers.

***

Aiden opened the gate. "Get Tok up and out if you can, E. I have to help Sissy."

Ethan picked up his shield, and it collapsed to a buckler. Then the little boy helped their new friend to his feet.

Aiden turned to catch up with Lauren, but the other cages at the edge of the camp caught his attention. Were

Mother and Father locked up in one of those cages? A thought flitted across his mind: *release them!*

He ran to the first cage, which contained exotic striped horses. From there, he could see that the next cage had colorful birds, a third had a large black cat, and the fourth a wolf. There was also a wagon with a wooden enclosure and barred windows.

He let the horses and birds out with a quick swipe of his sword, and they raced straight out of their cages, which opened facing the edge of the big tent.

They headed at full speed past Lauren and towards the guards. The guard on her left's attention was drawn away by the flurry of birds from the cage. Lauren's spear took him in the forehead, and he immediately crumpled to the ground, and the spear popped back into her hand.

That diversion was good, but it wasn't what Aiden had in mind. The animals ran past the side of the tent. *What if I can get the animals to run inside the tent?* Aiden looked at the big cat's cage. It faced the tent. He just needed to open the door just right.

He looked back to see Lauren lining up to throw her spear at the second guard. Before Lauren could make another throw, the guard did her the favor of tripping on his own feet and crashing to the ground as he passed out.

Aiden hollered as he pulled back his sword to swing it at the lock, "Sissy, run! I'm going to let this cat out."

She looked at Aiden with wide eyes and ran for the bear's cage. When she was well out of harm's way, Aiden cut open the cage and swung the door to channel the cat in the direction of the tent. The cat raced out like it was on fire. Seeing that the wolf cage was oriented the same way, he did the same with a similar effect. Next, he looked at the locked wagon and felt the call to *release them,* so he stepped toward it.

"Aiden, let's go!" Lauren called as the tent became an uproar of shouts and howls.

Aiden was torn. He felt he had to release whatever was in there. But they already got in way deeper than the scout he promised her they would do.

"Aiden, if we don't get out of here now, there will be consequences," Lauren insisted.

Release them crossed his mind one last time. He looked back at the wagon but couldn't really tell where its locks were. A pain-filled howl came out of the tent, and he knew the diversion wouldn't last much longer. *Uncle is probably right. It's not Mother and Father. The townspeople can save whoever it is when they come.*

"I'm coming, Sissy!" Aiden abandoned the wagon and raced to the others. He felt the heat in his heart diminish and the fire on the sword with it.

Ethan's shield was a beacon for Aiden as the flames on his sword had gone dark. Lauren joined Ethan in the cage.

"Hey, little guy, we need to go," Lauren said. Aiden heard voices mixed with feral animal howls from the direction of the tent.

"Bad man, make Bear hurt Tok." The little creature cried.

"I know, little buddy, but we fixed Bear." Lauren put her arm around him. "He won't hurt you anymore."

"Wake up, Bear?" Tok pleaded.

"You can try, but my spear usually knocks someone out for a long time," Lauren explained with little hope in her voice.

Tok shook the bear repeatedly to no avail. Aiden saw a spot of white near Lauren's feet. It was Meow Meow rubbing up against Lauren's ankles. *How had he gotten all the way out here?*

Lauren picked the kitten up and looked it in the eyes, "Do your thing," Lauren said, putting Meow Meow in front of the bear's face. The kitten licked the enormous animal's nose, and the bear woke with a start.

It winced as it put its injured paw down to stand up, but it seemed to lock eyes with Tok for a moment. Then it carefully stepped forward and nuzzled the diminutive Bjorn Born.

"C'mon, we've got to go." Aiden urged the group. They really had done a lot more than a scout, and if they didn't get out soon, it could be a real battle.

They helped the bear out of the cage and through the brush on to the path. Ethan's shield dimmed to just barely the light of a torch. Aiden was glad about that because he wasn't sure how they could navigate back to town without it.

They took longer getting to town than getting to the camp because of the bear's hurt paw. As they reached the edge of town, Tok said, "Tok. Bear. Home."

Aiden was dumbfounded by this. They'd just saved Tok, and now he was going to leave? How would Tok keep the bishop from recapturing the bear? "Are you sure you don't want to come with us?"

"Home." Tears were welling in the Bjorn Born's eyes.

"We understand; we'd like to be going home too." Lauren patted Tok on the shoulder.

"Tok, stay with us!" Ethan gave him a hug, and the bear let out a growl. So, Ethan stepped back.

"Tok sad." Tok sniffled. "Tok need go home. Tell family Bis'hop bad."

Aiden was surprised by this. "You mean the bishop came to your people?"

"Bis'hop bring red light." Tok nodded. "Make river clans bad. Tok tell family no red light."

"Sissy, we have to help Tok," Ethan begged.

"I just don't see how." Lauren shook her head.

"If I remember right, the Bjorn Born live in the foothills of the Iron Mountains. That's southeast." Aiden pointed in that direction with one arm. "We're going north." Then pointed in almost the opposite direction.

How could we tell Uncle any of this? I guess Tok is proof we didn't see a coon or a badger. But still, Uncle wouldn't want us headed into trouble. Aiden nodded in agreement. "There's no way Uncle would let us go with Tok to help his family."

Ethan frowned and looked down at his feet for a moment. "Sissy, pray!"

"Of course." Lauren put a gentle hand on Tok's shoulder. Aiden and Ethan did likewise, but this time the bear just nuzzled Lauren. "God, please watch over Tok. Keep him safe on his way home. Help him tell the truth to his people to keep them from the Darkness. Amen"

They all hugged Tok, and then he climbed on the bear's back, and they began to amble off to the southeast. Disheartened at his new friends leaving, Aiden led them to the hole in the stable.

They snuck back in, despite the exhaustion of the night's trials. Aiden had the presence of mind to put the straw bale back over the hole. He situated one feed sack on top of the other to make it look like it had before. Aiden was convinced that Uncle wouldn't be able to notice the extra board that was missing behind the bale.

Aiden felt like they had done some good in hurting the bishop's cause but was concerned that it wasn't enough. He

221

was sure they were disoriented and that if the townsfolk attacked in the morning like Uncle expected, they should win the day easily.

Sissy used the word consequences earlier. Knight Protector had said there were consequences when you didn't heed the 'still small voice.' What consequences would there be for not opening the wagon? He still felt a strong urge to go back and let whatever was in there out. Hopefully, the townsfolk would do it.

As he drifted off to sleep, he realized that the red light leaving the camp was going to the north. Did the bishop know they were here? He had to if the bald boy was the acolyte. Was there a trap being laid for them on the road ahead? How could he warn Uncle without letting on about their adventure?

32. Precious Cargo

Refi'cul woke to a boot in his back. "Get up. Master's got work fer you to do, now!"

The rough treatment didn't do anything for the vile mood he'd fallen into just before bed. *Those evil kids! When I find them, they will know my wrath.* He had just been settling into eating at the bishop's table when the yells went up from outside. Then the giant cat came storming into the tent, followed by a wolf. The tent came down on top of him! The rest was a blur that ended with him sleeping on the ground in the open.

So much for the bishop's promise of 'revels.' What does he want now? It's not even morning yet, and my face is killing me. Another boot to the back, "Alright, alright already, I'm up. You kick me again with that boot, and I'm going to make you eat it."

He rolled over to his knees and looked up to see the bishop. "Oh, your excellency. I'm so sorry. I didn't realize…."

"Enough, boy!" the bishop stood with his hands on his hips. "We have no time for your groveling." You must be off now. I sent out a patrol after the battle last night, and they have returned with news that the townsfolk are on their way here in force. Without Skull Crusher, this could be a close battle."

The bishop pointed at the wagon. Aiden didn't open, "I need you to be on your way with that wagon to fulfill your mission in the Iron Hills before they get here."

"Why the wagon?" Refi'cul protested, "Wouldn't I move faster without it?"

The bishop backhanded him in the cheek with the bear claw wound, sending searing pain through Refi'cul's skull. "Don't question me, boy! Those prisoners are to go with you to the Iron Hills and be locked away in its deepest dungeon."

Fearing another slap, Refi'cul turned his face to protect the wounded side, "If you would please forgive me for my impertinence, Your Holiness, but who are they?"

The bishop shook his head, "The fact that you have to even ask makes me question if you can fulfill the destiny put before you."

Now Refi'cul was genuinely conflicted. He desperately wanted to know who he was transporting to the Iron Hills, but at the same time, he didn't want to further anger the bishop.

The bishop let out a huff, "You really haven't figured it out, have you?"

Refi'cul shook his head and looked down at his feet. He couldn't tell if the burning in his cheeks was from shame or from the slap.

The bishop put his hand on Refi'cul's back and shoved him in the direction of the wagon, and they began walking toward it. "It's the children's parents, you dolt. It was by the power of the Dark One himself that they weren't released last night with the animals."

Refi'cul looked up at the bishop, "Their parents! Why don't we kill them now?"

The bishop shook his head, "They haven't yet outlived their usefulness."

Refi'cul wondered what that meant but felt it was important to just listen as the bishop continued, "All will be revealed once you have usurped the throne of the Iron Hills."

They reached the wagon, which was lit with light from two lanterns. Patches and three other horses were hitched to it, and his pack was sitting on the driver's seat. The bishop motioned Refi'cul to get in. "When my purposes are complete, you can have the honor of slaying these heretics. For now, you must ensure they are safely locked away in the depths of the Iron Hills."

A deep sense of anticipation came over Refi'cul, "It will be my pleasure."

33. Question of Faith

The children woke to the rumble of wagon wheels and the patter of rain sprinkles on canvas over them. Lauren attempted to sit up only to realize Uncle had put the canvas over them low and tight like when they'd first come into town.

The boys woke up as well, and Ethan yelled, "Coo Coo, we're locked in here. Can we get out?"

"Rain's gonna come up pretty strong by the looks of it," Uncle called from the driver's seat of the wagon. "You'll stay dry in there."

A moment later, he added, "There's vittles in the sack there. Just relax. We got out of there just in time."

Lauren scooted closer to the wagon seat so she didn't have to yell, "What do you mean?"

"As we were leaving, the townsfolk were gathering at the inn with axes and pitchforks plannin' to go after the bad element in the woods," Uncle explained. "That wasn't trouble we needed. So just settle down, and I'll open up the tarp when the rain stops."

"Yes, sir," Lauren replied to the children as she contemplated whether to talk to Uncle about their adventure the night before. *Consequences* kept bouncing around in her head like the bumps on the road.

The day passed on without incident other than Uncle having to get off the wagon a couple of times to dislodge it from a muddy rut. In the early afternoon, the rain stopped, and Uncle pulled back the tarp. Lauren took this opportunity to read the Good Book aloud. There was a story about a prophet of the Lord having a contest with five hundred of the Dark One's priests. In the end, God gave the prophet holy fire, and the evil priests were defeated.

***

As evening came, Uncle found a suitable place, and they stopped to camp for the night. They sat around the fire after dinner, keeping the chill off from the damp air.

The cougar hide had dried enough, and Uncle began sewing it into his cloak so the head was at the top of his hood.

Uncle asked, "That good guy in the story you were readin', did you say he was a prophet or a parson?"

This was the first time Uncle had shown any awareness of them reading the Good Book. Lauren paused for a moment to choose her words carefully, "Well, in those days, a prophet and a parson were the same thing, I guess. The land was overtaken by the Darkness. The temple, we'd call it a church, was full of these bad priests." Lauren could tell by Uncle's intent look he was hanging on her every word, "But God gave the prophet the message he wanted the people to hear, just like he does with a parson. Why do you ask?"

"Well seems like the story you just read is pretty much what happened in Loggerton, according to the parson." Uncle grabbed the coffee pot.

"Seems the Darkness people came into town preachin' some new thing that got everybody all excited. Once they took over, the parson got thrown in the lock-up fer hateful talk, they said." Uncle paused as he poured his coffee. "Then late one night, about a week ago, the parson convinced his guard that he had a message from the Lord to give to the priests in the middle of their late-night services."

Lauren noticed the boys leaning in to hear the conversation.

Uncle continued, "Anyhow, the dark ones had some kind of wild ceremony. The parson said when he walked in, there was some hell hounds surrounding a censer and their leader. He heard a loud horn call, and that all disappeared. He called them out on being with the Dark One just like that prophet did in yer story."

Uncle pointed to the Good Book, "Apparently, the parson called out to the Lord just after midnight, and suddenly every one of them censers they had, exploded in a flash of light."

"When did you say this was?" Lauren asked expectantly.

Uncle looked up and off to the right and paused for a moment. "Would have been the night before I picked you up."

"That was when the tower at our house made the censer explode," Aiden blurted out.

Uncle did a double take, "What's this yer talkin' bout now?"

"Uncle, I know you have a tough time believing us, but everything we told you before was real." Lauren stood up and took a deep breath.

Uncle stared back at her across the fire in silence but gave the slightest of nods.

"The cougar had the Darkness in it somehow," Aiden cut in. "Our weapons got their powers, like when we fought the bishop."

Lauren put up a hand, hoping Aiden would get the hint to let her do the talking. Uncle's intense gaze told her he was seriously considering what they were saying. She knew she was threading a needle with this conversation. "When God wants us to help fight evil, our weapons get power."

Ethan jumped up. "Yeah, like last night. Tok needed help, and we saved the bear and broke the bad men's tent."

"You did what?" Uncle exclaimed, his eyes getting a wild look. Red rushed into his face.

No! Ethan, why'd you open your mouth? This is going to be a mess. Lauren attempted to diffuse the situation. "The creature we told you about was a Bjorn Born. The dark ones had captured his bear, and he needed help freeing it. Our weapons activated, so we knew we needed to help."

Uncle stood up, clenched his fists, and began to pace, looking at Lauren with clear anger in his eyes. "When I saw the mud on the hem of the boys' pants and a couple of briars on yer skirt, I chalked it up to being in a dirty stable. But now you're telling me you left the stable and didn't tell me? What did I tell you kids about blood being thicker'n water?"

The hurt look on his face made the children feel ashamed of themselves. Uncle went over and picked up the Good Book.

"Yer pa was always Good Book this and that. It's clear that's all gone to yer heads." Uncle pointed at the kids with the Good Book. "Where in this does it say kids can go coon huntin' all night when their uncle says, 'sit tight, things are dangerous'?" Uncle asked accusingly. "I know enough of what's in here to know yer supposed to mind yer elders and not be lyin' and sneaking around."

Uncle glared at them.

I knew we should have gotten him to help us. He was starting to believe. Now things are worse.

"I'm so sorry, Coo Coo," Ethan blurted out as he began to cry.

"Right now, I don't want to hear it." Uncle turned his back on them. "You get to bed. I don't want to hear another word out of yer dishonest and disrespectful mouths."

Lauren hung her head in shame in silence as she and the boys got ready for bed. She lay there, unable to sleep. What consequences would come of their betrayal?

34. Troll Bridge

The next morning came with a literal fog that overshadowed the heavy mood from the night before. Uncle said little other than an occasional order during breakfast and packing up. Lauren felt there would be no reconciling with him this morning, so she whispered encouragement to the boys to do their best diligently and silently.

In the fog, Uncle didn't get on the wagon and drive like he normally did; instead, he got out in front of the horses on foot and walked them. As noon came, the fog finally burned off, but the sky remained dark. Uncle took his seat in the wagon. "I was planning on being on the other side of the Zoura river before dark. There's a way-stop there with a well and a trading post."

"That's a good idea, Coo Coo." Ethan patted Uncle on the back.

"Uncle, the word is *Uncle*," the big man corrected while looking forward at the road. "Ya ain't a toddler no more. Learn to say it right."

Ethan's lower lip quivered, and tears began to form in his eyes.

Lauren silently put her arm around him, and her compassion stifled his tears. Lauren looked at Aiden, whose squinted eyes and pursed lips told her he was angry with Uncle for putting Ethan down. She put her index finger to her lips to keep him from possibly making things worse.

Uncle continued without looking back, "As I was sayin', to get where we're going, we'll have to drive on past dark and eat in the wagon."

"Yes, sir." Lauren wondered if the rest of the trip would be under this haze.

***

As they moved north, the day seemed to get darker and darker. A starless night came upon them two hours early. *This is like at the church the other day. How do I tell Uncle about this?*

There was an unusual chill in the air, and Uncle put on his cloak. Aiden put Daddy Duck's box over the duck and put Meow Meow under it, too, hoping they would share warmth. The children wrapped up together in a blanket.

Uncle lit a torch and attached it to a holder. The flickering light played off the cougar skull, making Uncle a truly fearsome sight. He picked up his axe and put it across his lap before he proceeded.

He senses it too. He just won't admit it. She checked the weapons for a sign of light, but they weren't glowing at all. *Maybe it's just the weather, after all.*

By the time they reached the crossroads at the southern end of the bridge across the Awoi River, it was pitch black. Torches extending every ten feet down the hundred-yard length of the stone bridge were barely providing enough light to see the path.

Uncle pulled up short in the middle of the crossroads so suddenly that the horses veered off to the right, stopping diagonally in the intersection.

He laid Ol' faithful on the driver's seat and got off the wagon, torch in hand. He motioned Lauren over to him.

"Somethin' ain't right," he whispered as he grabbed Ol' Faithful off the driver's seat and hung it on his back.

"What, Uncle? What should we do?" A knot settled into Lauren's stomach. She scanned their weapons tied to the side of the wagon for a sign that wasn't there.

"*We* ain't gonna do anything," Uncle said. "There's two watchmen and what looks like a toll man over there. They weren't here last time I came through."

"Is there any way I can help?" Lauren offered despite expecting another rebuke.

Uncle looked around the area. "You get up in that driver's seat and take the reins. If this goes sideways, I want you to get these horses moving while I get in the back. Got it?"

"Yes, sir." Lauren complied but then turned to watch him as he approached the toll man. The hair on her arm stood up, and her skin prickled. She couldn't determine if it was from the chill or also an indication that trouble was about to meet them.

***

Uncle approached the toll man's tent and rang the bell. Then he turned to look at the guards by the bridge. Their slouched posture and dusty appearance led him to believe they were just farmhands or day laborers pressed into service. Their conical metal helmets were dinged and showed signs of rust. They had single-bitted woodmen's axes leaning against the bridge and daggers in their leather belts. The only oddity was their black-on-black uniform of a linen shirt and denim pants, and black boots. They weren't well kept, but it represented a uniform he'd never seen before.

He heard someone's throat clear and turned to find a man in the same uniform but with a chain mail shirt and a deep-red feathered plume coming out of his helmet. He was standing behind the toll desk.

"Evenin', Sergeant. What's all this about?" Uncle said, pointing his torch towards the bridge. "This is Freeman's way. No toll to be taken here."

"Lieutenant! I'm a Lieutenant, you uncouth savage." The officer put his hand on the hilt of his sword.

"Hey now, no offense meant, Loo'tenant. I just ain't never seen yer outfit before." Uncle tried to diffuse the situation. He looked over his shoulder quickly and saw the guards had stiffened to attention and were now headed his way. Uncle scanned the surroundings quickly and didn't see any other guards, but there were three horses tethered to the bridge post nearest him.

235

"Very well," the Lieutenant said. "We're no highwaymen here to rob you. We are border security."

"Border security? Since when's Awoi and the Heathlands got a problem?" Uncle asked.

"Since the Darkness has been spreading like the plague from the north. There are reports that some are fleeing Loggerton to their stronghold in the north," the Lieutenant retorted, bending slightly to put his hands on the table between him and Uncle. "Papers? I need to see your papers."

Uncle had never had any papers, not in his whole life. The guards had arrived now and flanked Uncle two steps to his rear. Then he remembered the writ for the children. With all the seals, he could probably use that as papers. "They're in my bag. Be right back."

He turned and almost ran into the guard on his left. "Beg Pardon." Then he went to the wagon. The Lieutenant's story made sense. Uncle lowered his guard some as he approached the wagon.

"What is it, Uncle?" Lauren asked expectantly.

"Just the militia keeping the bad guys from using the bridge," Uncle explained as he reached for his travel bag.

"Oh, that's good then." Lauren brightened as she shivered.

"Go get back in that blanket before you catch a cold," Uncle offered with the slightest bit of warmth in his tone. It was hard to stay mad at the nibbles. They were right about The Darkness being real. It was just hard to admit it being a dyed-in-the-wool skeptic.

"Thank you, Uncle." Lauren climbed into the back of the wagon and snuggled down with the boys. As Uncle retrieved the writ, he left Ol' Faithful on the buckboard.

"Uncle," Lauren whispered. "Look! Ethan's shield is glowing."

Uncle turned and stared at the shield. It seemed like a trick of the torchlight to him. The color was a bit off, like a blue-white hue. He looked over at the toll man and saw him tapping his fingers on the table. "We don't have time for that nonsense right now," Uncle whispered. "This is gonna be touch and go as it is." He returned to the toll man's table.

"You are the brother of the signatory?" the lieutenant asked as he pointed to the signature on the paper.

"Yes, sir," Uncle said.

"The children are in the wagon?" the Lieutenant pointed at the wagon.

Uncle turned and noticed the guards moving toward the children.

When he turned back, he felt the tip of the lieutenant's dagger at his neck. "Don't move!" the lieutenant ordered. "One twitch out of you, and the children die."

Uncle stiffened. *Not my nibbles! Not today!* He stared into the toll man's eyes, "You sure that's how you want to play this?"

At that, Ethan's shield shone with its full glory, illuminating the crossroads. The lieutenant pulled the hand, holding the dagger back to shade his eyes. Uncle seized the initiative and brought his torch down on the other man's head, stunning him and catching the plume on fire.

Uncle grabbed the writ off the table and turned to run for the wagon, torch in hand. His jaw dropped, and he stopped short at the sight of the three children standing in the back of the wagon, holding their weapons with holy light surrounding them.

As the first guard reached the wagon, Lauren threw her spear at him. It trailed watery blue light as it flew. When it connected, the man dropped unconscious. Then the spear reappeared in her hand.

Uncle was stuck in place, dumbfounded. *That can only be the Light! They weren't telling fairy stories.*

The second guard swung at Aiden. Ethan blocked the axe blow with his shield. As the axe bounced off harmlessly, Aiden cut the axe head off with his flaming sword. Lauren followed through with the point of her spear to the assailant's temple, and he crumpled unconscious to the ground.

Uncle heard a bugle call behind him that was cut short as Lauren's spear passed over his shoulder. He heard the thump of the lieutenant dropping to the ground. The spear popped back into Lauren's hand. *I just saw it, but I can't believe it. They took out the whole squad in seconds.*

"Come on, Uncle! We need to go!" Lauren waved to him.

Uncle looked down the torch-lit bridge, assessing whether to proceed north as planned or detour to Quinn's Ferry. *If we go to Quinn's Ferry, that knight protector will be there, and I'll have to eat crow.*

Despite his years of experience as a woodsman and fighting all manners of beasts, his jaw went slack when he saw a giant begin stalking across the bridge from the far side. He had heard of the Heath Wardens before but always thought they were a tall tale. *I guess crow's gonna be on the menu.*

"Lauren! They have a Heath Warden!" Uncle pointed toward the advancing foe. "Get you and the boys out of here, now! Head east to Quinn's Ferry."

"Uncle, we can beat him." Ethan was brandishing his shield in the air.

Uncle paused. *Could they really do it?* Lauren's spear strikes had been dead on every time. Only the Light could give a little boy the power to cut clean through an axe.

Uncle looked back down the bridge; the giant had already cleared half of it. Now that he was closer, Uncle could see it was wearing some kind of harness and had some black iron contraption on his back that was spewing black smoke into the air. *I don't know what that is, but it can't be good.* He realized he was still holding the writ in an iron grip and shoved it into his waist pouch. Then he tossed the torch where he thought it might best light the battle and pulled Ol' faithful off his back.

"Lauren, when he gets close enough, try yer spear." Uncle felt a tingle go up his spine and down his right arm. He looked at his hand, and it seemed like Ol' Faithful had taken on the blue glow of Ethan's shield.

Must be seein' things. He shook his head and turned back to the advancing giant.

"Is that three little children playing warrior, I see?" the giant bellowed as he strode across the bridge. "Hopefully, they will be more of a challenge than their father was when I captured him! Even now, he's locked with his wife safely away at the bishop's camp. When this is done, the whole lot of them will be entombed in the Iron Mountains." The giant paused to let out a horrible laugh.

"Oh no! I left them locked up!" Aiden cried in anguish. Uncle turned and saw the fire in Aiden's sword flicker out. At this, Uncle's stomach clenched, and the tingling sensation left him. "Lauren, you need to get that wagon moving."

He scanned the area around him, preparing for battle. He saw that the soldier's horses were still tied up to an iron ring attached to the right main support for the bridge. He moved to the ring.

"I can do this, Uncle," Lauren let loose with her spear as the giant came into range. It flew true straight for the

240

giant's head. Just as it was about to impact the giant, the black smoke from the thing on its back swirled in an egg-shaped dome around the giant. The smoke deflected the spear, but the giant still staggered and fell to one knee. The spear popped back into Lauren's hand.

"Hah!" the giant bellowed. "Three little children are no match for Skull Crusher. They will fall as their father did. The bishop will be pleased."

Uncle froze. *With all their talk of the Light, that giant's something else entirely. They don't have what it's gonna take. I don't have it, either, but I can give the nibbles a head start.*

Uncle held Ol' Faithful in his right hand near the head and waved it at the children. "Kids! Get that wagon moving! Now!"

Uncle saw tears in Aiden's eyes as he stared blankly at his sword, which was no longer flaming. Ethan peeked out from behind his shield, "Coo coo, we can beat him. We have to shine our light."

"No, *we* can't." Uncle unhitched the horses from the ring while the giant gained his feet. Then he swatted the horses' rumps and sent them running headlong down the bridge toward the giant. The giant barely got out of the way of the first, only to be knocked back to his knees by the second and third.

Uncle rushed back to the wagon. "Lauren, get the boys to Quinn's Ferry." Then he swatted his own horses to get them moving. As the wagon passed him, he swung his axe to cut Clarabelle loose to keep her from slowing them down.

As the wagon careened off into the darkness, Uncle turned to face the giant. He realized the giant wasn't going to be intimidated by his cougar pelt, and the cloak was likely to get in his way. He threw it off to the side. He took up a two-handed combat stance with Ol' Faithful just as the giant cleared the end of the bridge.

"Ain't no man nor beast layin' a finger on my kin while I draw breath."

The giant laughed. "I am neither man nor a beast. I am of the Nephilim of old. I am the Skull Crusher. Yours will be easy enough." The giant readied his war hammer, and Uncle charged. *God, if you are real, give me the strength to hold off this monster till my nibbles are safely away.*

35. Wild Ride

When the wagon jerked forward, Lauren heard a loud thump behind her. However, it took all of her strength and focus to keep the horses on the road.

Ethan's shield provided enough light around the wagon for Lauren to follow the path, but she had little real control over the beasts. After two miles of frenzied racing, the horses were exhausted and slowed to a walk. Lauren pulled to a stop.

"Sissy! We have to go back and help Coo Coo." Ethan cried out as the light in his shield faded to nothing.

"Aiden? Should we go back?" Lauren asked as she turned around in the driver's seat. "Aiden! Why won't you answer me?"

The night was pitch black, except for a faint glow on the horizon to the east. It was not like the tower or a torch, but a break in the overcast sky, where Lauren could barely make out the road creating a rise. She couldn't see anything in the wagon.

Ethan's hand touched Lauren's arm in the dark. "Aiden conked his wonkus when the wagon took off."

"Oh no! Not Aiden too!" The bottom dropped out of Lauren's stomach at the thought of Aiden being seriously injured, especially after Uncle's apparent sacrifice. Tears began to well in her eyes.

"Lauren, Sparkle Frog helps head eggs. Maybe he just has a head egg. Help me find him." Ethan began patting things in the wagon as he tried to find Sparkle Frog's bucket.

Lauren joined him, and in the process, they knocked over Daddy Duck's box. In the darkness, the duck didn't startle to fly away. He merely flapped his wings and let out a big quack. Something about the white spot on his forehead made it stand out like a beacon.

After some more casting about, Ethan found Sparkle Frog's bucket knocked over, but the lid was still shut tight. When he pulled the frog out, it seemed the spot on Daddy Duck's head reflected light in the frog's iridescent back.

Lauren found Meow Meow curled up next to Daddy Duck. When she picked him up, his white spots seamed to interact with the other two pets to lighten the wagon ever so slightly. In that pale light, she found Aiden unconscious but alive.

Lauren gently nudged him out of the awkward position he had fallen into and onto his back. Ethan immediately put Sparkle Frog on the bump on his brother's forehead. As expected, the lump went away. However, Aiden didn't awaken. Lauren put Meow Meow on his chest, and the kitten nuzzled Aiden's chin.

His eyes fluttered, and he groaned, "What happened?"

Lauren pet Meow Meow's back. "Uncle scared the horses, and they ran off fast. When they finally calmed down, the light in E's shield went out. We want to go help Uncle, but I can't see enough to drive the wagon."

Aiden sat up and rubbed his head. "Where's my sword?"

"I don't know, Aiden. I saw it fall into the wagon." Ethan responded. "I'll help you find it."

Lauren heard the boys casting around in the back of the wagon but couldn't see much more than some vague shapes moving. *Consequences. Not again. Why does that keep going through my mind?* This time she knew. She saw the light start in Uncle's axe and then disappear. Deep down, she felt it was their dishonesty that caused him to falter. If only they'd introduced him to Tok. He would have believed. *Now there's no light to save him.*

Tears began to form in her eyes. "Aiden, Ethan, I love Uncle as much as you do. But I'm not sure God wants us to go back."

"But, Sissy, I know we can beat the giant," Ethan begged. "We just need to shine our light."

"With what Light?" Lauren shook her head as the tears streamed down her face. "The power is gone."

"It's all my fault, I was supposed to let Mama and Daddy out, and I ran away." Aiden cried. "I didn't listen to the 'still small voice.' Now, Uncle's gone too."

Lauren cast around until she found Aiden and put an arm around him, "It wasn't just you, Aiden. I didn't listen either and let us run off without bringing Uncle. If I wasn't in such a hurry to get back, you might have finished the job." The two of them sobbed in silence.

"Sissy, it's so dark it's like we're in the belly of the big fish. Is this our big fish?" Ethan asked and then clamored through the back of the wagon. He grabbed Lauren's hands and folded them together, "Sissy, pray." Ethan's unwavering faith brought Lauren a ray of hope.

Lauren bowed her head and prayed, "Father God, we know we didn't listen to the voice, and we're sorry. Please show us what to do. We love Uncle and want to save him. But we don't want to disobey his wish for us to be safe. Please show us the way."

Daddy Duck flew as high as the cord would let him and gently flapped his wings to stay in the air. He let out a quack as if to say untie me.

"Aiden let him fly," Lauren urged. "I think it's a sign."

"Sissy, what if he flies away? In the dark, he can't find his way back," Aiden said in a quivering voice. "We've lost so much. I don't want to lose him too."

Lauren hugged Aiden, "Daddy Duck lit the way to save Sparkle Frog and to destroy the Darkness machine. I think he'll shine the way out of this."

"OK, Sissy." Lauren could feel Aiden casting around to find where the cord was tied.

"I found it." Aiden rolled away from Lauren to use both hands on the cord. Then Daddy Duck rose, and a narrow beam of light suddenly shot out from the south. It hit the white spot on Daddy Duck's head and bounced a beam of light onto the ground where the duck looked.

The light passed over the children, and Lauren felt her stress and weariness melt away. The light passed over the horses, and they stopped panting and stood taller. The duck then flew to light the path towards Quinn's Ferry.

Despite the calm that had washed over her, Lauren felt a pang of defeat. "Boys, this is a pretty clear message. We need to go on like Uncle said."

"But…Coo Coo?" Ethan said with his lip quivering.

Lauren hugged Ethan. *Do I tell him about the light I saw on the axe? How do I explain that it disappeared?* "We just have to pray that God will keep him safe. Maybe he gave him power like the strong man when we left."

Aiden climbed into the driver's seat and urged the horses on. All night long, it seemed they could never reach the brighter horizon before them. It seemed like the deep darkness kept moving in the direction they were.

***

Skull Crusher could sense the dawn coming in the east more than he could see it. The censer seemed to call to him to conceal it. In his haste to capture the children, he couldn't gather his pack. The big man's cloak was the only form of concealment he had.

He was starting to panic when he found a thicket of bushes. They were on the west side of an overhanging hill. He saw a hollow in the bushes where he could put the censer and lie down. Recognizing that the censer would be safe, he let out a sigh, and the tension in his shoulders released.

With a grunt, he placed the censer and its harness under the overhang. His legs were like jelly from the long run, so he collapsed next to the censer. For a moment, all he could do was stare toward the darkness in the west. Feeling more than seeing the oncoming dawn, he roused himself. The giant spread the cloak over the bushes.

The censer's fumes began to build under the cloak and dulled the pain from where he had cauterized the wounds he'd taken from the big man. He hated that the big man had fallen from the bridge. He hated that the only skull to harvest from the battle was the cougar skull on the cloak.

The only thing he hated more was that the bishop would be furious with his failure to deal with the children at the bridge. It had been months of building the censer network to reach striking distance of the Aowi river bridge. His mission was to secure the bridge and kill the children. In chasing after the children, he had failed both.

When he was sent on this mission, he couldn't imagine why the bishop cared so much about three tiny human children. After being attacked with the glowing spear, he understood the threat they posed. Now, nothing was going to stop him from tracking them down. He would wait out the daylight and catch them in the night.

***

As dawn came, the brighter horizon finally seemed to be growing nearer. When they reached full daylight, Daddy Duck descended to land on Aiden's head. Aiden set his friend on his box, and the duck tucked his head under his wings and fell asleep. *You rest now, good buddy. You've earned it.*

They had traveled at high speed for hours now, and despite the earlier refreshment, the horses and children needed a break. Aiden pulled them off the road, and the children took time to water the horses in the river.

Aiden took this opportunity to really see what was going on behind them. A mile or so back, the sky was a dark haze that continued getting darker toward the bridge. *That doesn't really make sense. All night long, the light stayed about the same distance ahead of us, then it just stopped. Why?*

"I'm so glad we're finally out of the darkness." Lauren put a hand on his shoulder. "Maybe that's why God had us keep going. There was too much darkness there for us or something."

"Or maybe Knight Protector was right, and we're supposed to go to Blooming Glen to fight the Darkness better." Aiden pointed to the road. "This is the road to Quinn's Ferry that can get us across the river on the way to Blooming Glen."

Ethan piped up, "Didn't Knight Protector say if we got in trouble, we should go there?"

It made sense, but the Darkness moving to follow them bothered him. *If we wait too long, will it catch back up with us?* Aiden turned to look Lauren in the eye, "So, do we keep pushing the horses?"

"God helped us last night, but we were in the Darkness. I think we should take a nap and move on this afternoon," Lauren suggested.

Aiden thought about it for a minute. *The Darkness stopped moving at daylight. If we move some today, we should be able to stay ahead of it.* "OK, but not for too long."

After feeding and watering the horses and nibbling on some hardtack, the children lay down in the back of the wagon as best they could. Noon came and went, and it was three o'clock before they roused themselves.

"How did it get so late?" Lauren asked as she sat up.

"We need to get going." Aiden jumped down from the wagon to get the horses.

"Sissy, I'm tired. Can't we just stay here some more?" Ethan whined.

"Go back to sleep. Aiden and I have this." Lauren tousled his hair.

The older children got the horses reattached to the wagon, and by the grace of God, neither one had lost a shoe or gone lame in some way. However, based on the stress of the previous day, the children decided to drive at a slow walk.

Twilight began to fall in the east as they came over a small hill. On the other side, the road descended a gentle slope for another mile to the banks of the Muddy River. The path they were on intersected Saint's Road going north and south, and just to the south was a small village. Directly ahead were docks and a ferry boat, as well as a two-story wooden trading post and inn. The inn at Quinn's Ferry.

"Sissy, I think that's it." Aiden pointed excitedly.

Lauren woke Ethan up and tried to fix his hair. Aiden couldn't believe that she would worry about his hair after all they'd been through.

As the sun finally fell, Aiden stopped the wagon in front of the inn. His eyes went wide at what he saw in front of him. Knight Protector was sitting in a rocking chair on the veranda, visiting with an elderly woman.

He got up. "Children? Is that really you? Where's your uncle?"

"Coo Coo fought the giant and made us go." Ethan cried as he jumped down from the wagon and ran to the man. "I shined my light, but Coo Coo made me go."

Knight Protector took a knee and let Ethan hug him around the neck. "A giant, you say?"

Aiden got down and tied up the horses while Lauren addressed Knight Protector's questions. "Yes, Uncle called him a Heath Warden. He carried a censer on his back, and my spear didn't work on him."

"The enemy is adapting," Knight Protector said as he put a hand on his shoulder. "I'm sorry about your uncle." Ethan let go of Knight Protector, and the man stood and put his hands on Aiden's shoulders. "I'm sure your uncle was doing what he thought was right."

"We know," Lauren stammered. "It's just if he only believed."

"We must all make that choice, child." The knight turned to Lauren. "Did you see him fall?"

The other children just shook their downturned heads.

"Then, there is hope. Your uncle is a powerful man, like your father. He may have won through."

Aiden appreciated Knight Protector's kind words. Uncle was very brave to fight the giant on his own to protect them. *How do I tell him that I left Mama and Daddy with the bishop? If Daddy had been there, they would have beaten the giant for sure.* Lacking the words to say, he shook his head with deep regret in his heart.

"Now, children, come in and get some dinner." Knight Protector motioned to the elderly woman. "This young lady sets the best table in Quinn's Ferry."

"Oh, hush now," the old woman said as she leaned on her cane to stand up. "Come on in, and I'll send the stable boy for your horse and wagon."

"But what if the giant comes?" Ethan looked around nervously. "We need our weapons."

"There is a whole platoon of the Mighty Mercenaries' best marines here in the inn," Knight Protector said. "I anticipated if you redirected to Quinn's Ferry, you might be bringing trouble with you."

"But . . ." Ethan began.

"Just in case," Aiden said, ignoring the knight, and vaulted into the back of the wagon. He handed the shield to Ethan and the spear handle to Lauren. He picked up his sword, willing the light to come, to no avail. *Would the fire come back again?*

"Very well." Knight Protector ushered the children into the inn.

They sat at the table, and food was brought. "Children, I promised to get you safely to Blooming Glen, and I mean to do it. There may be more danger ahead, but for tonight you can rest easy."

"Sissy, pray," Ethan said as he caught his sister about to put a buttered biscuit in her mouth.

She set it down and folded her hands. "God, please bless this food and the hands that made it. And please, dear God, keep Mama, Daddy, and Uncle safe."

Allen Brokken

36. Epilogue

The geese landed gracefully in the dawn light. One on either side of the waterlogged figure floating on driftwood in the Awoi river. Their platinum feathers reflected the light all around them, making the area as bright as noonday. Each goose swam to a shoulder and ducked its head under an arm. They lifted their heads and pulled the big frontiersman up off the driftwood.

They floated with him down the river, where it met the great Muddy River and on to Francis Ford. There they slowly waddled up onto the shore with their charge in tow. Once he was out of the water, they put their heads down and walked back out from under his arms. Then the geese patiently waited.

As the sun reached noon, the man's eyes opened. He slowly sat up on his elbows, and his eyes were dazzled by the glorious light reflected from the geese. A wave of peace and healing flowed over the man. "I'm still drawin' breath, so ain't no giant gonna hurt my nibbles."

To be continued… in <u>Fear No Evil</u>

If you enjoyed Still Small Voice, please share your review.

<u>Good Reads</u>   <u>Amazon.com</u>

Acknowledgments

A book like Still Small Voice takes a tribe to make it happen. I found my tribe at the <u>Realm Makers Consortium.</u> To make it real, I'd like to thank the following people for their contributions to Still Small Voice.

Sarah Grimm
LoriAnn Weldon
J.J. Johnson
Kalyn Cummins
Jennifer Darst
Brice Spencer
Jason Perryman
Gen Saint Martin
Scott Minor
Jason Joyner
Elisabeth Warner
Angela Anderson
Wendy Blanton
Anna Tan
Beth McMillion
Leam Hall
Elizabeth Kitchens
Elisabeth Warner
Gretchen Kuykendall Engel
Katie Clark
Claire Banschbach
Lee James

About the Author

Allen Brokken is a teacher at heart, a husband, and a father, most of all. He's a joyful writer by the abundant grace of God. He began writing the Towers of Light series for his own children to help him illustrate the deep truths of the Bible in an engaging and age-appropriate way. He's dedicated 15 years of his life to volunteer roles in children's ministry and youth development.

Now that his own children are off to college, he's sharing his life experiences on social media, at home school conferences, and through his blog, occasional cool dad projects, and the Silly Celebrations newsletter at https://towersoflight.net/subscribe

You can get sneak peeks of the ongoing adventures of Lauren, Aiden, and Ethan (plus their pets!) regularly and the #dadjokeoftheday on all the major social media platforms.

@allenbrokkenauthor

Towers of Light Series

The series insightfully examines Christian values from the perspective of three small children facing insurmountable problems and succeeding by faith and grace alone.

Book 1: ***Light of Mine***- *Discernment*
The Darkness has taken their parents. Can Lauren, Aiden, and Ethan discern who to trust before it takes them too?

Book 2: ***Still Small Voice*** – *Conscience*
Lauren, Aiden, and Ethan want to follow their conscience to save their parents, but their Uncle has other plans. Will he see the light before it's too late?

Book 3: ***Fear No Evil*** -*Courage*
Lost and alone in a valley of Darkness, will Lauren, Aiden, and Ethan find God's courage to find redemption and each other?

Book 4: ***Armor of God*** – *Faith*
Lauren, Aiden, and Ethan race across the Heathlands on a quest to arm themselves with the Armor of God. Will their faith give them the power to save their father?

Book 5: ***Wellspring of Life*** – *Redemption*
Lauren, Aiden, and Ethan must find the legendary wellspring of life. Will they be able to share its living waters before it's too late?

Book 6: ***Demolishing the Stronghold*** – *Victory*
Lauren, Aiden, and Ethan reach Blooming Glen only to find the city defended by the Dark One's Forces. Will they have the faith to overcome the enemy and Light the Tower?

Looking for quality literature for language arts?

New Classics Study Guides

offers free literature units for homeschooling. This is a curated collection chosen by a veteran homeschool curriculum provider, Phyllis Wheeler of MotherBoardBooks.com. The authors have banded together and created study guides for their books. Explore the links to find your next new classic for your child's literature unit. Download for free!

newclassicsstudyguides.com

Made in the USA
Columbia, SC
28 April 2023

15589814R00162